NICK CARTER
FANTÔMAS

A Play in 5 acts and 8 scenes

by

Alexandre Bisson and **Guillaume Livet**

translated and adapted by

Frank J. Morlock

A Black Coat Press Book

Acknowledgements: We are indebted to David McDonnell for proofreading the typescript.

This book is dedicated to Al Segal, my classmate, friend, and doctor for many years of friendship.

Nick Carter was created by John R. Coryell from a story by Ormond G. Smith.
Fantômas was created by Pierre Souvestre and Marcel Allain.

Visit our website at www.blackcoatpress.com

Nick Carter:
American-Made, Internationally-Loved

The undisputed king of template characters—that is, archetypal popular culture characters who are widely imitated—is Sherlock Holmes. Holmes imitations, copies, lifts, pastiches and homages number in the hundreds. But what is not widely appreciated is that, until 1939, he had a close competitor: Nick Carter.

Nick Carter first appeared in 1886 (a year before Holmes) in *"The Old Detective's Pupil; or, The Mysterious Crime of Madison Square"* (*New York Weekly*, September 18, 1886). As written by his creator, John Russell Coryell, Carter is a young private detective in New York City. He was raised by his father, the famous private detective Old Sim Carter, to be as great a man and crime-solver as possible. Toward this end, Sim began training Nick when he was a boy, putting him through a series of physical and mental tests, so that Nick is not only capable of lifting "a horse with ease…while a heavy man is seated in the saddle," but also is knowledgeable in every area that might conceivably have to do with crime-fighting, from the sciences to various languages to art to physiology. Carter is only 5'4"/1.625m tall, but is well-muscled, grey-eyed and handsome.

As an adult, Carter is acclaimed as the greatest private detective in the United States. He has the respect of the police, who regularly consult him, and is admired by the public. His cases often require him to travel around the United States and the world, but he maintains a healthy set of relationships with his family and assistants. In his first appearance, he marries Ethel Dalton, and she remains a semi-regular character in the series, until she is killed in 1904.

Carter soon acquires an assistant, Patsy Murphy, a bootblack who becomes a full-fledged detective. Murphy marries a beautiful South American woman, Adelina de Mendoza, and she becomes one of Carter's most valuable agents. Murphy eventually gave way to Carter's second, and permanent, sidekick, Chickering "Chick" Valentine, a teenaged Nevada ranch hand who is Carter's physical double. Carter adopts Valentine, who takes Carter's name, and Chick begins helping his adoptive father solve crimes while also working on his own as a detective.

Carter's cast of supporting characters changes and evolves over time, and includes the brilliant schoolgirl Ida Jones, the Japanese detective "Talika the Geisha Girl," "Ah Toon," the royal detective to the Emperor of China, and "Ten-Ichi, the son of the Mikado."

Carter's enemies are among the most colorful and varied in popular culture. He takes on ordinary kidnappers, blackmailers, murderers and Black Hand/Mafia thugs, but he also has a Rogues Gallery of unusual opponents, including the sociopathic vivisector Dr. Quartz (a Hannibal Lecter *avant la lettre*), the beautiful Russian princess and deranged criminal mastermind Dazaar, the Arch Fiend Praxatel of the Iron Arm (detective fiction's first cyborg) and Princess Olga, the tiger chief of the

Russian Nihilists. Nor are Carter's stories always mysteries. In one story, Carter discovers a lost race of mixed native and Viking descent in the Andes. In another, he finds a hidden city in the Tibetan Himalayas, whose inhabitants are masters of "vibrational science" and can channel vibrations to kill others. And in a third tale, Carter encounters a race of superhuman Bolivian Amazons who intend to conquer the world.

The passing of time was slowly acknowledged in the Nick Carter saga. Characters grew older, married and had children. The children of enemies Carter defeated appeared as adults to fight Carter. And Carter himself aged incrementally, from 18 during his debut to mid-thirties by the end of the series. Events from previous stories were acknowledged in later tales, including references to Carter's two wives (both dead) and to previous encounters with individual villains.

Carter's character evolved to match the changing literary environment. When Carter debuted, he was a standard dime novel detective who was described as brilliant, but whose conclusions were reached with the help of the author and the plot, and whose crime-solving relied on brawn as much as brain. But within a decade after Carter's debut, Sherlock Holmes had become popular in the United States, and Carter changed and became like Holmes, a brilliant consulting detective who solved cases through inspired deductions. In the 1920s and 1930s, Carter became a typical pulp private detective, losing most of his supporting cast, his wealth and his personal history, and relying more on his fists than his brain to solve crimes.

Carter is a working private detective, and charges for his services, but he is primarily motivated by a desire to see that justice is served; his stated goal is to "aim for the right and righting wrongs." He is resolutely honest and moral and never gives in to temptation; his only vices are beer and the occasional cigar. But while Carter's sympathies are always with the victim, he is not interested in social restructuring, and his stories contain no sustained critique of authority. Members of the establishment are occasionally portrayed as criminals, including corrupt bankers and politicians, but generally the resolution of a story leads to the restoration of the social *status quo*, with the criminal members of the establishment portrayed as aberrations rather than the inevitable byproduct of power. In the Nick Carter tales, crime is an individual failing and an isolated event, rather than an indication of a social problem. In this regard, Carter, although a crime fighter, is a defender of the establishment rather than the individual.

Nick Carter's longevity and popularity made him influential on other detective characters. His origin is similar to Doc Savage's, and several elements of Carter's approach to detecting, from his multiple disguises to his methods of contacting his band of agents, were used by The Shadow. Carter used a number of gadgets, including spring-loaded revolvers and high-powered explosives, which were adopted by numerous pulp and comic book characters.

Carter's popularity manifested itself in another way: through global imitation. The first pulp magazine was *Argosy*, which began being printed on cheap wood pulp paper (from which the term "pulp" derives) in 1891. At the turn of the century, pulp publishers began turning away from the general fiction format of *Argosy* and began publishing single-genre pulps, and, in imitation of the dime novels, single-character pulps. In 1905, Street and Smith, which had been publishing Buffalo Bill stories in various dime novels since 1869, sold the license to those tales to several European publishers, and they began selling translations of those. French and German readers were not unfamiliar with serialized adventure fiction–the *colporteur* and *feuilleton* predate the American novella and dime novel–but the stories of Buffalo Bill were written at a more basic literary level, without any attempts at literary worth, with an emphasis on melodrama and action, and in the genre of frontier fiction, which was the most popular genre of popular literature of the time. As importantly, each issue was relatively inexpensive.

The Buffalo Bill tales were immediately popular. The following year a German publisher began selling copies of *heldromans* ("hero-novels," or the German equivalent of the pulps) about Sitting Bull, and these were just as successful. Cheaply-printed and affordable magazines about both men appeared across Europe and sold well everywhere. Imitations of both characters appeared in European countries and in Russia over the next decade. In the years leading up to the beginning of World War I, other characters from American pulps and British story papers became popular enough to spawn European imitators or unauthorized sequels, with Sherlock Holmes, Sexton Blake and Fu Manchu leading the way.[1]

But with the exception of Sherlock Holmes, none of these characters were as successful or popular as Nick Carter. Carter was, of course, hugely successful in the United States, appearing in more than 4,000 stories in 20 magazines (including nine bearing his name and devoted

---

[1] One such imitator, *Harry Dickson: The American Sherlock Holmes*, will be published by Black Coat Press in 2008.

primarily to his adventures) between 1886 and 1939. Street and Smith sold the license to Nick Carter to European publishers in 1906, and reprints of those tales, and an uncountable number of unauthorized sequels, appeared across Europe, Russia, Asia, Central and South America, the Middle East and North Africa until 1939.

But an equal indicator of Carter's popularity was the speed with which he was turned into a template character, and the number of countries which made use of him in that fashion. There are a handful of template characters in popular fiction: Sherlock Holmes (the Great Detective, the brilliant consulting detective), Arsène Lupin (the gentleman thief with *joie de vivre*), Philip Marlowe (the cynical, hard-boiled private detective), The Shadow (the costumed vigilante) and a few others. Nick Carter's template is a variation on Holmes'. Like Holmes, Nick Carter is a Great Detective. But Nick Carter stories have as much action and adventure as they do deduction and crime-solving, so that the Carter template is a character equally formidable with his brains and his fists. Holmes could handle himself in a fight, but he was not regularly involved in brawls, as Carter was.

As well, Sherlock Holmes is so identified with England, and London, that most Holmes imitations were English characters whose adventures took place in London. In contrast, Nick Carter regularly travels around the world, so that although he is American, he is far more mobile than Holmes. Because of this, the Carter template was easily transposed on characters from other countries and cultures. It is this aspect that separates Carter not just from Holmes, but also from Sexton Blake. Blake had a large number of imitations, but, like Holmes, most of them were English and located in England. Blake's physical side is derived from Carter, so in a sense Blake can be seen as a Nick Carter imitation. So too is Nat Pinkerton, who was an extremely popular character in Europe, Scandinavia, Russia and the Middle East from 1907 to 1933 and inspired his own set of imitations. Pinkerton is named after Allan Pinkerton, the head of the Pinkerton Agency, and runs a Pinkerton-like detective agency, but in every important respect Nat Pinkerton is based on the Nick Carter template.

A brief survey of some of the international characters modeled on Nick Carter:

• In Czechoslovakia, there was Jaroslav Pulda's Leon Clifton, who appeared in *Z Pamětí Amerického Detektiva Léona Cliftona* #1-275 (1906-1910), and Harry Ward, who appeared in *Z Pamětí Amerického Detektiva Harry Warda* #1-6? (1925).

• In Denmark, there was Fasmer, created by Robert Storm Petersen and Axel Breidahl and appearing in *Kobenhavn ved Nat* #1-10 (1913), and *Kobenhavn ved Nat* #1-6 (1941), and Dick Donald, who appeared in *Dick Donald, Mesterdetektiven* #1-8 (1942-1943).

• In France, there was Paul Garbagni's Nick Winter, who appeared in nine films between 1911 and 1921, as well as pulps in Spain (1912) and Turkey (1918), and Jean-Charles Lagaillarde's Dick Cartter, appearing in *Dick Cartter, le Roi des Détectives* #1-21 (1924).

• In Germany, there was: Robert Heymann's Pat Conner, who appeared in *Pat Conner, der Meister-Detektiv* #1-30 (1908), a series which was reprinted across Europe, Scandinavia and Russia from 1908 to 1915; John Wilson, who appeared in *John Wilson, Aus dem Geheimbuch des berühmten amerikanischen Detektivs* #1-56 (1908-1910) and in an Austrian pulp in 1909 and a Russian pulp in 1910; Jack Franklin, who appeared in

Jack Franklin, der Meisterdetektiv #1-41 (1911) and in a Danish pulp in 1918; Stuart Webbs, created by Joe May and Ernst Reicher and appearing in 50 films between 1914 and 1930; Joe Morris' Will Morton, who appeared in *Kleine Detektiv-Romane* #1-370 (1919-1927) and in a Danish pulp in 1923; Walther Kabel's Nic Pratt, who appeared in *Nic Pratt, Amerikas Meisterdetectiv* #1-33 (1922-1923); and Manfred Schmidt's Nick Knatterton, which has appeared in an eponymous comic strip in the *Grünen Post* from 1935 to the present.

• In Hungary, there was Galantai Gyula's Tom Pick, who appeared in *Tom Pick a Detektiv Király Kalandjai* #1-36 (1910-1912); Doctor Kubb, created by the pseudonymical "Nick Carter Kiadó" and appearing in *Doktor Kubb a Világjáró Érdekfeszitö Kalandjai* #1-46 (1922-1925); and Uránia Kvny's Hungarian detective Nick Carter, who appeared in *Magyar Nick Carter* #1-4 (1926).

• In Italy, there was Joe Petrosino, who appeared in *Giuseppe Petrosino* #1-100 (1909-1910) and similar series in Germany, Italy and France, and Harry Sander, who appeared in *Harry Sander. Il Poliziotto Mondiale* #1-20 (1930).

• In the Netherlands, there was Maciste, who appeared in *Maciste de Schrik der Bandieten* #1-28 (1919), and Jack Jackson, created by J. Davids and appearing in four novels between 1922 and 1925.

• In Norway, there was Sven Elvestad's Knut Gribb, who has appeared in more than a thousand stories and dozens of novels from 1908 to the present. (Gribb began as a whitewashed Nick Carter clone but gradually became his own character).

• In Poland, there was Stefan Wenke, who appeared in *Stefan Wenke, Słynny Warszawski Agent Śledczy* #1-20 (1908), and Joe Deebs, created by Joe May and appearing in 28 films in Germany between 1915 and 1920 and the Polish pulp *Joe Deebs, Najsilniejszy Człowiek i Najlepszy Detektyw na Świecie* #1-5 (1924).

• In Portugal, there was Jim-Joyce, created by Reinaldo Ferreira and appearing in at least 60 stories between 1926 and 1928, and Ralph Williamson, also created by Reinaldo Ferreira and appearing in "Novas Aventuras de Ralph Williamson" (*Magazine Bertrand*, 1927-1928).

• In Spain, there was Jack Ford, who appeared in *Jack Ford. El Terror de los Malhechores* #1-16 (1912); Ros-Koff, who appeared in *Aventuras del detective Ros-Koff* #1-5 (1913); John Sanford, who appeared in *Episodios Policiacos. John Sanford* #1-32 (1916); Robertson, who appeared in *Robertson. El As de los Detectives* #1-42 (1930-1931); and Steel Fist, who appeared in *Puño de Acero* #1-10 (1932).

• In Sweden, there was Harry Strong, who appeared in *Kapten Ströms Berömda Bragder Och Reseävntyr* #1-2 (1908), and Julius Pettersson's Maurice Wallion, who appeared in a number of stories and 12 novels and short story collections from 1916 to 1924.

• In Turkey, there was Ebüssüreyya Sami's Avni, who appeared in a number of stories and ten issues of an eponymous dime novel from 1910 to 1920; İskender Fahrettín Sertellí's Yilmaz, who appeared in a dime novel series and three novels from 1925 to 1928; and Nermi's Cemal, who appeared in *Yıldırım Cemal'in Büyük Muvaffakiyetleri* #1-4 (1928).

In the 1940s and after, Carter became an unexceptional private detective, and in the 1960s and after, he became a James Bond knockoff. Today, Nick Carter is mostly forgotten, while the affection for Sherlock Holmes remains unabated. But, for several decades, Carter was Holmes' main rival, and this should not be forgotten.

Jess Nevins

Characters

Nick Carter
Melvil (a.k.a. Fantômas)

in order of appearance:
Judge
District Attorney
Bobby Paddock
Mr. Davis
Mr. Morgan
Bailiff
Helen Dodler
Margaret Dodler, *her aunt*
Sergeant-at-Arms
Jim
Sam
Arizona Jack
Patsy Murphy
Chick Carter
Catherine
Messenger
Carmen
Deborah
First Upholsterer
Second Upholsterer
George Clancy
Mrs. Morris
Mr. Morris
Mr. Van Burg
Hotel Groom
Harry Pelham
Meltcraft
Francis

Oswald
Williams
Pedro
Tomato
Tippett
Otto
Jacoby
Vampira
Sweets

The play takes place in New York in January 1910.

ACT I

Scene I. The Trial

A courtroom seen from an angle. To the left of the stage, the Judge's bench. In front it, two tables: one for the D.A. and his assistant, another for the accused and his attorney. Behind them, another table, for the members of the Press. To the right of the Judge's bench, the witnesses' stand and a door leading to the Judge's chambers. To the left of the Judge's bench, against the back, the Jury's box and another door, for the Jury and the accused. To the right, two rows of chairs, divided by a central alley, for the public, which enters from the far right, and a large window.

Melvil and Bobby Paddock are seated at the table for the accused, with their attorneys, Messrs. Davis and Morgan. Melvil is somberly handsome and elegantly dressed; Bobby, dressed more casually, has a cheery and bright face. Arizona Jack, dressed as a cowboy, is seated in the front row with Helen and Margaret Dodler. Jim and Sam are seated further back amongst the public. They wear exactly the same clothes as Melvil and Bobby, to whom they must bear the greatest possible resemblance. They hold their coats folded over their knees.

Three policemen stand guard, watching Melvil and Bobby. The journalists are scribbling their notes at their tables. The trial has just begun.

DISTRICT ATTORNEY: (*standing, continuing his speech*) Such, Gentlemen of the Jury, is the man who appears before you today. Always searching for a dupe or a victim. Thanks to his strange powers of seduction, he beguiles the friendship of some and the confidence of others. He has used all kinds of disguises; changed his name and appearance as easily as his domicile. He moves with extreme ease from the most luxurious hotels to the most sordid of dives where crooks and rogues gather. A single word will suffice to fully enlighten you as to his character: this so-called Mr. Melvil, this formidable malefactor, is as intelligent as he is audacious–

MELVIL: (*haughty and ironic*) You overwhelm me–

D.A.: –He deserves to be called by his alias: The King of Crime–Fantômas!

(*The Judge is taken by a fit of coughing.*)

BOBBY: (*low to Morgan*) The Judge's got a fine cold.

D.A.: This is the third time that this man has fallen into the hands of the Law. Arrested for burglary eight years ago, he escaped prison by corrupting two of his guards. The following year, he robbed and killed the banker Wilson, and was caught again. However, when the police van arrived at its destination, the murderer was no longer inside–but the body of the policeman charged with watching him was! Finally, only last month, Melvil and his accomplice, Bobby Paddock, (*Bobby bows slightly*) at night scaled the wall of the home of Miss Helen Dodler, entered her room and carried her off. But they were arrested by the most celebrated of detectives, Nick Carter–

BOBBY: (*low*) Ah, that brute!

D.A.: –Who then tied them up and turned them over to the police. This time, all precautions have been taken. The bandits have been unable to escape, and we expect you will do them good and prompt justice. (*To the Judge*) May Your Honor be kind enough to call the first witness?

JUDGE: Bailiff! (*A new fit of coughing*)

BOBBY: It breaks my heart to hear him cough like that.

JUDGE: (*after he stops coughing*) Bailiff–call the first witness for the Prosecution.

BAILIFF: (*calling*) Miss Helen Dodler!

HELEN: (*rising*) I'm here!

MARGARET: (*excited, restraining her*) No, don't go, Helen, don't go!

HELEN: But I have to, Auntie!

MARGARET: I don't want you to leave me!

(*Laughter in the audience.*)

HELEN: Look, Auntie, this is ridiculous.

MARGARET: I don't want you to go near those bandits–that monster with a human face.

(*More laughter. The Judge bangs a small silver gavel for the noise to cease.*)

SERGEANT-AT-ARMS: Silence, down there!

BAILIFF: (*going to Margaret*) Don't be afraid for your niece, Mrs...

MARGARET: (*correcting him*) "Miss," if you please! (*To Helen*) Be careful, Helen! Don't go near him! Walk around him!

BAILIFF: Come, Miss Dodler.

(*Helen follows the Bailiff, who escorts her to the witness box. As she passes near Melvil, he rises and bows to her respectfully.*)

JIM: (*low to Sam*) Say, Catherine isn't here.

SAM: (*scanning the public*) No, I don't see her.

JIM: (*low*) I wish she were here!

JUDGE: Miss Dodler, do you swear to tell the truth, all the truth and nothing but the truth?

BAILIFF: (*presenting Helen with a book which he holds in his hands*) Swear on the Bible.

HELEN: I swear it. (*The Bailiff returns to his table.*)

D.A.: Please sit down, Miss Dodler, and answer the questions I am going to ask you. Your name is Helen Dodler, and you live with your aunt, Miss Margaret Dodler, in a house located on 5th Avenue?

HELEN: Yes, sir.

D.A.: You're an orphan. Your fortune, which is said to be considerable, is administered by your god-father, Mr. Harry Pelham, an old friend of your father?

HELEN: Yes, sir.

D.A.: How often do you see Mr. Pelham?

HELEN: I haven't seen him since he settled in France, in Normandy, seven or eight years ago. But we write each other frequently and he's promised to be present at my marriage.

D.A.: You are engaged?

HELEN: Yes, sir.

D.A.: Do you know the accused, Mr. Melvil, here present?

HELEN: I knew him under the name of Robert Huntington.

D.A.: (*pointing to Melvil*) But he's actually the same man? You are certain of it?

HELEN: Absolutely certain.

D.A.: How long have you known him?

HELEN: Around a year, on and off. I spent a few weeks in Boston at the home of one of my friends. The day after my return to New York, I saw Mr. Huntington for the first time, when he came to take tea with us. During my absence, he was introduced to my Aunt Margaret, whom he had met at a charity ball.

D.A.: Did he come to your home often?

HELEN: Once or twice a week at first, then his visits became more frequent.

D.A.: What was his attitude toward you?

HELEN: Oh, very correct! Mr. Huntington showed himself very friendly and showed me great consideration; his conversation was most brilliant, his wit most amusing. And I confess that, at first, I was very happy with this new friendship.

D.A.: And then?

HELEN: And then–not so much.

D.A.: May I ask you why?

HELEN: (*a bit embarrassed*) Because Mr. Huntington, who had seemed until then more particularly occupied with my aunt–

MARGARET: (*protesting*) For goodness' sakes! That's untrue! That's untrue! Such a scoundrel–

(*Laughter in the auditorium.*)

BOBBY: The old maid's getting mad. (*laughs*)

MARGARET: (*hearing him, furious*) Old maid!

BOBBY: She's mad because she wasn't the one being carried off!

(*More laughter.*)

MARGARET: Look, Helen, you know it's untrue. You cannot believe–this, this malefactor! Never! How dare you say such a thing!

HELEN: But, Auntie, I swore to tell the truth.

(*More laughter. The Judge bangs his gavel.*)

BAILIFF: Silence!

HELEN: Anyway, I soon noticed that Mr. Huntington made himself more officious–very officious indeed–in my regard. His attentions multiplied, his gallantry accentuated; in short, he became annoying. One day, I was forced to remind him bluntly that I was engaged and his out-of-place insistence offended me. He bowed, without saying a word in reply; then, he withdrew and completely ceased his visits.

D.A.: You didn't see him again?

HELEN: No, sir.

D.A.: Until the night of January 14? What happened to you on that night?

HELEN: Oh, I remember very little about it. I was sleeping; I was suddenly awakened by the light of a lantern shining in my face. I wanted to scream, but someone placed a kerchief soaked in chloroform over my face, and I lost consciousness. When I came to, I was stretched out in the salon, surrounded by my aunt, a doctor and my maid, who apprised me of the odious kidnapping attempt of which I had almost been the victim–and from which I escaped, thanks to the cleverness and courage of Mr. Nick Carter.

D.A.: You didn't see the face of the man holding the lantern?

HELEN: I didn't see any faces. Everything appeared to me in a flash of light. Only later did I learn of Mr. Huntington's guilt.

D.A.: It surprised you?

HELEN: It pained me deeply.

D.A.: Do you know his accomplice, Bobby Paddock?

HELEN: No, I don't know him.

BOBBY: (*gallantly*) The sorrow is all mine.

D.A.: Thank you, Miss Dodler. (*To Davis*) Mr. Davis, does the Defense desire to question this witness?

DAVIS: I do! I will first ask the charming witness–

MELVIL: (*rude, authoritative*) Shut up!

DAVIS: Why–?

MELVIL: I do not allow you to question Miss Dodler.

DAVIS: Pardon me! I am responsible for your defense, and my duty as an attorney–

MELVIL: Enough!

DAVIS: (*sitting down*) Fine! As you please! So much the worse for you.

JUDGE: You can step down, Miss Dodler.

MARGARET: Come, Helen, let's leave. Let's get out of this awful place. It's stifling.

(*Margaret leaves through the door at the right. More laughter. The Judge raps his gavel again.*)

BAILIFF: Silence!

JUDGE: Bailiff– (*He has another fit of coughing.*)

BOBBY: You've got a nasty cold, Your Honor.

JUDGE: Bailiff, call the next witness.

BAILIFF: (*calling*) Mr. Nicholas Carter.

(*Curiosity among the public.*)

ARIZONA JACK: I don't see my friend Nick Carter.

BAILIFF: (*calling louder*) Mr. Nicholas Carter!

(*Nick enters from the right, followed by Chick and Patsy.*)

NICK: I'm here!

(*Exclamations from the audience. They press around him and all rise to see him.*)

JIM: There he is!

ARIZONA JACK: (*letting out an echoing yell*) Whoop! Hello, friend!

NICK: (*shaking his hand*) Hello, Jack! Calm down! Don't shout so loud.

SAM: (*low to Jim*) The dirty rat! Ah! If I had him alone in some dark place–

JIM: (*low*) You wouldn't get very far. It's he who'd have the best of you.

(*Chick and Patsy sit next to Arizona Jack. Nick has reached the witness' stand.*)

ARIZONA JACK: Hello, Chick! Hello, old Patsy! How's it going?

SERGEANT-AT-ARMS: Quiet down there, cowboy!

NICK: (*to the Judge*) Will Your Honor please excuse me for arriving a bit late?

JUDGE: You're not late at all, sir; you are very punctual. You've arrived at the exact moment when we need you! Will you be so kind as to take the oath? Do you swear to tell the truth, all the truth and nothing but the truth?

NICK: (*placing his hand on the Bible that the Bailiff presents to him*) I do!

(*The Bailiff returns to his seat.*)

JIM: (*low to Sam*) Catherine's still not here!

D.A.: (*to Nick*) Sit down, Mr. Carter and, for the record, tell us your name and your profession.

DAVIS: (*rising, to the Judge*) Pardon me, Your Honor. By addressing such a question to a man as well-known as the witness, the Prosecution hopes that the name of the illustrious Nick Carter will raise enthusiastic acclamations and prejudice the Jury against my clients...

D.A.: Not at all! It's the law!

DAVIS: (*ironic*) –But far be it from us to oppose such a declaration! To the contrary, we willingly stipulate that we completely share the opinion of the District Attorney, and with him, we proclaim that Mr. Carter is the most celebrated, the most astonishing detective in the entire world. He's marvelously gifted man, brave to the extreme, whose reputation is unassailable.

NICK: (*smiling*) That's too much! That's too much!

DAVIS: And we sincerely admire his exploits, that we do not hesitate to qualify as legendary, since they appear to exalt fiction more than reality.

NICK: How flowery!

DAVIS: In short, we recognize Mr. Carter as one of the glories of our age and country.

NICK: (*mockingly*) You are another, Mr. Davis!

(*Laughter, applause and uproar in the public, amongst which can be heard a resounding "Whoop" hurled by Arizona Jack.*)

JUDGE: (*banging his gavel*) If these demonstrations continue, I will have the courtroom cleared! (*Followed by another fit of coughing.*)

BOBBY: (*to Morgan*) He'd better clear his chest!

JIM: (*low to Sam*) It's all going to go wrong if Catherine doesn't come.

SAM: (*low*) Don't worry, she'll come.

D.A.: (*to Nick*) Do you know the defendant, Mr. Melvil, here present?

NICK: (*smiling*) Yes, I know him. We've crossed paths several times before. In fact, I dare say we do know each other very well indeed.

MELVIL: (*haughty and ironic*) And we appreciate each other.

NICK: He's a villain of the most dangerous type: without conscience, without fear, cunning, with uncommon strength and sharp intelligence.

Truly, there's a certain degree of pleasure in measuring oneself against such an adversary.

MELVIL: You are going to make me blush!

NICK: Almost a shame that such a fine career should be so near its end.

MELVIL: (*threatening*) Who knows? Perhaps we may yet meet again.

NICK: That's not very likely! Burglary, murders and a kidnapping are more than enough to warrant the sternest punishment.

MELVIL: Bah! Carter, you are a pessimist.

D.A.: For the moment, we are only concerned with the kidnapping. Do you know the Dodlers?

NICK: Yes. They are kind enough to honor me with their friendship.

D.A.: Will you tell us how you came to help them on the night of January 14?

NICK: Gladly. At the beginning of the month of January, I met the Dodlers. I had not seen either of them for some time, and they informed me that they had a new friend, Mr. Robert Huntington, a most distinguished gentleman— and most seducing. Miss Margaret, especially, couldn't stop praising him and I remember that we exchanged a few jokes on the subject. Some days later, Miss Helen, who is interested in photography, showed me a picture of Mr. Huntington, that she had taken unbeknownst to him. There, I immediately recognized the formidable Fantômas, whom I'd fought before. My stupor was great, but I didn't allow it to be seen in order to not cause the Dodlers any alarm. However, I promised myself to watch over them. Two days later, Miss Helen told me that, during her last meeting with the so-called Mr. Huntington, she'd been forced to tell him to go away, and that since then, he hadn't reappeared at their house. However, I knew this man well enough to be certain that he wouldn't let go so easily of such a tempting prey! So, I asked my two assistants, Chick and Patsy, to increase their vigilance. I ordered them to shadow the wretch. Ah, he's a wily antagonist, full of audacity and very resourceful. Finally, on January 14, Patsy said to me: "I think there'll be some action tonight. Bobby Paddock, Melvil's henchman, was seen around the Dodlers' mansion this afternoon, inspecting the windows and sizing up the walls. Let's get ready." Indeed, towards 2 a.m., Melvil and Paddock arrived in a carriage, harnessed to a horse whose hooves had been wrapped in fabric. They got into the mansion, carried off Miss Helen, but were arrested on the spot by myself, Chick and Patsy.

ARIZONA JACK: (*rising*) And me, friend Carter, you've forgotten me.

(*Laughter in the courtroom.*)

NICK: That's true. The brave Arizona Jack was with us.

ARIZONA JACK: I was the one who knocked out the driver. Whoop! Whoop!

(*More laughter. The Judge bangs his gavel. Order is restored.*)

NICK: After having bound and gagged them, we took Melvil and Paddock to the Tombs, where they were the object of special attention, and all precautions were taken to prevent them from escaping.

D.A.: Do you know the other accused, Bobby Paddock?

NICK: A thief and a blackguard whom no one would want to meet at night in a dark alley.

BOBBY: Now, that's how reputations are made! Ah! You're not nice, Mr. Carter! As for me, I always spoke well of you!

NICK: And a drunkard, too!

BOBBY: For goodness' sake! For the last two months, I've only drunk water!

NICK: They don't give you alcohol in prison?

BOBBY: No! Can you imagine? It's a scandal!

D.A.: I thank you again, Mr. Carter, Mr. Davis, your witness. (*He sits down.*)

DAVIS: (*rising and speaking in an ironic tone*) I will dare ask a few questions, with all the respect one owes to such a great man, naturally.

NICK: (*smiling*) By all means! Don't stand on protocol!

DAVIS: Just now, you said that you were sure that Mr. Melvil would return to the home of Miss Dodler, because, as you put it, "he wouldn't let go so easily of such a tempting prey." I believe her fortune is estimated to be in the neighborhood of 15 millions?

NICK: So?

DAVIS: According to you, Mr. Melvil, in acting as he did, was only motivated by the money–and the money alone. Is that your opinion?

NICK: Wouldn't that be yours, too, Mr. Davis?

DAVIS: So you see no other motive, which might have driven him to commit the action with which he is now charged?

NICK: (*smiling*) I see. You mean love, perhaps? Some kind of mad passion?

DAVIS: Why not?

NICK: Fantômas in love? The King of Crime singing to the starry sky while picking daisies?

DAVIS: He's a man like any other.

NICK: Come on, you can't be serious?

DAVIS: It wouldn't be the first time that a man lost his head over a woman. And you will concede that Miss Helen is dazzling enough to justify such an attempt.

NICK: I suppose it was your client who floated that ludicrous explanation?

MELVIL: (*haughty*) I haven't confided in anyone.

NICK: (*to Davis*) So you discovered this all by yourself? I cannot compliment you on it.

DAVIS: You will grant me that my client's reserve doesn't help your cause. A doubt remains.

NICK: Not for me.

DAVIS: And it also seems to me that if Mr. Melvil were only looking to despoil Miss Dodler, he would have burglarized, not kidnapped her.

NICK: What about her ransom? You're forgetting the ransom! It's a classic case of kidnapping.

DAVIS: (*lightly*) But collecting a ransom can be dangerous–and not very practical. And, frankly,
sordid, very sordid. Not at all my client's
style.

NICK: You think so?

DAVIS: On the other hand, kidnapping is an easy means
of elopement that lovers have always em-
ployed and is in favor more than ever. Certainly, I do not approve of it. I will even con-
demn it, if I must. But is it entirely inexcus-
able when you risk losing the woman you
adore forever? Because, Gentlemen of the
Jury, it must not be forgotten: Miss Helen
has a fiancé; her marriage is approaching;
therefore, there was a need for my client to
act promptly and energetically–

NICK: Just a minute! One small observation, if I may. It
wasn't Miss Helen, it was Miss Margaret, her
aunt, that your client was initially courting–
and I suspect that his passion was motivated
by–

DAVIS: How do you know that Mr. Melvil wasn't trying to please the aunt, solely in order to get
closer to her niece?

NICK: He didn't know her then.

DAVIS: How do you know that?

NICK: Ask him.

MELVIL: (*breaking in*) That's my business, and what I think is nobody else's business.

DAVIS: It's in your interest to make it known to the Gentlemen of the Jury.

MELVIL: I'm not concerned about the Jury. What I've decided will be done. That's all I have to say.

DAVIS: Still–

MELVIL: (*curt*) Move on.

JIM: (*low to Sam*) The Boss is magnificent!

DAVIS: Well, in any event, as I said, a doubt remains and such reasonable doubt must indeed benefit the accused. I put it to you, Gentlemen of the Jury, that this so-called kidnapping was nothing more than a matter of passion.

(*Davis sits down. Catherine enters from the right and sits on a bench. She is around 50 and is made up outrageously, like a young girl.*)

JIM: (*low to Sam*) Ah! There's Catherine!

MORGAN: (*rising*) I beg the witness to let us know what he thinks the role of my client, Bobby Paddock, was in this affair?

BOBBY: Yes, that's interesting.

MORGAN (*to Bobby*): You'd do better to shut up

NICK: (*always in good humor*) Gladly.

BOBBY: (*to Morgan*) But I can't remain here doing nothing!

MORGAN: In my view, he merely lent a hand to a friend to help him win the heart of the one he loves–

NICK: You call that winning her heart?

MORGAN: That's not an unforgivable crime.

NICK: It's a mockery.

MORGAN: (*raising his voice*) In Ancient Greece, wasn't Pirithous famous for helping his friend Theseus carry off Helen, daughter of Leda?

(*Nick and the whole audience are stupefied.*)

BOBBY: (*to Nick*) That shuts you up good, huh?

MORGAN: Why, then, make a crime of Bobby's good nature when Pirithous wasn't reproached for it?

BOBBY: Yes, why? Always two weights and two different measures?

MORGAN: In our days, as in ancient times, friendship has its duties.

BOBBY: That's for sure! (*smiling with satisfaction*) Pirithous!

MORGAN: And one must think twice before accusing my client of complicity when what he did was nothing more than help a friend.

BOBBY: (*triumphantly*) There you go!

JUDGE: Is that all you have to ask the witness?

BOBBY: (*with enormous pride*) Pirithous!

(*Laughter in the courtroom.*)

JIM: (*laughing*) Sonofagun, Bobby. "There you go!"

MORGAN: I beg your pardon, Your Honor, one more word. (*To Nick*) I would like to know whether it was Mr. Melvil or Mr. Paddock who was the first to enter the Dodlers' mansion!

NICK: It was Melvil.

MORGAN: That is quite important, Gentlemen of the Jury. Mr. Melvil went in first, so therefore my client can't be accused of breaking and entering, since the door was already open–

NICK: The window, actually.

MORGAN: It's the same thing. Door or window, the essential thing is that it was already open, therefore there was no breaking and entering, merely a trespass. All that remains is the so-called kidnapping, then. Mr. Carter, did my client brutalize Miss Helen?

NICK: No, I never said that.

BOBBY: (*indignant*) Me, harm a woman!

MORGAN: Was it he who applied the chloroform?

MELVIL: It was I!

BOBBY: I was only holding the candle.

MORGAN: Who was it who carried Miss Helen in his arms?

NICK: Melvil.

MORGAN: In that case, Gentlemen of the Jury, my client, Mr. Paddock, did nothing more than accompany his friend and light his way. The crime which he might have committed is merely that of trespass, and the wrongdoing slight.

NICK: (*smiling*) I don't know if Pirithous lit the way for his friend Theseus, but you have a way of presenting things in a colorful fashion, Mr. Morgan. Ah, this is not banal! Do you have any more questions for me?

MORGAN: (*sitting down*). No. Thank you, Mr. Carter.

NICK: (*to the Judge*) May I be excused then, Your Honor? We are presently engaged in an important investigation, and every minute counts.

JUDGE: You use your time too well for this Court to wish to waste it. You are free to go, Mr. Carter.

NICK: Thank you, Your Honor.

(*Nick exits right, accompanied by shouts of "Long live Nick Carter!" and Whoops from Arizona Jack.*)

JIM: (*low to Sam*) Luckily for us, he's gone.

SAM: (*low*) Watch for the signal! As for you– (*He exchanges a glance with Catherine.*)

JUDGE: Bailiff– (*Another coughing fit.*)

BOBBY: What do you take for your cold, Your Honor?

JUDGE: (*threateningly*) Shut up, Mr. Paddock.

BOBBY: I was merely asking, Your Honor, because I know a good remedy.

JUDGE: (*between coughs*) I'm going to have you sent back to jail.

BOBBY: Right! Right! Don't get mad. I'll shut my trap!

JUDGE: Bailiff, call the next witness.

BAILIFF: Mr. Patsy Murphy.

PATSY: Here!

(*Patsy arrives at the witness' stand*.)

BOBBY: (*to Patsy, as he passes near him*) Hello, Patsy, old boy. How's it going?

PATSY: Hello, Bobby.

JUDGE: Do you swear to tell the truth, all the truth and nothing but the truth?

PATSY: I do!

D.A.: Would you tell us your name and profession?

PATSY: Patsy Murphy, private detective, working for Mr. Nick Carter.

D.A.: Do you know the accused, Mr. Melvil?

PATSY: Yes, I do. He's a scoundrel, the leader of a gang of thieves and sharpers.

D.A.: You were at Mr. Carter's side on the night of January 14?

PATSY: Yes, and I helped him to the best of my ability.

D.A.: Do you have more details to give us on the subject of the attempted kidnapping?

PATSY: Not much! While Mr. Carter was taking control of Mr. Melvil, wrestling him to the floor and cuffing him, I was busying myself in the same way with Mr. Paddock.

BOBBY: No hard feelings, old boy, but you really played pretty rough! I was all black and blue!

PATSY: (*laughing*) So did you, Bobby! A bit more effort and you'd have strangled me!

BOBBY: (*protesting*) Oh, for goodness' sake, I'd never do that! Box, yes, fisticuffs, as much as you like, but murder between us–never!

D.A.: Were you previously acquainted with Mr. Paddock?

PATSY: I've known Bobby since my childhood. We're both Irish. We grew up together in Galway.

BOBBY: Oh! Those were the good old days! You remember old Mrs. Bradbury, with her cat and her parrot?

PATSY: We left the old country on the same day, on the same boat, and came to America to seek our fortune. There, we grew apart from each other.

BOBBY: A question of taste! But when we meet, we fall in each other's arms, right Patsy?

MORGAN: (*to Patsy*) Since you know my client so well, do you think he's capable of decent feelings?

PATSY: Hum! Hum!

BOBBY: (*nobly*) Ah, Patsy, that doubt offends me!

MORGAN: See, Gentlemen of the Jury, my client is not a hardened criminal. Perhaps he drinks more than he should, and the company he keeps is abominable, but don't you think he is entitled to some leniency?

PATSY: I don't know what to say.

BOBBY: (*offended*) My dear chap, I understand perfectly well you don't want to give me your sister's hand in marriage, but all the same, I've never killed anybody.

PATSY: The truth is, he's not altogether bad–at heart.

BOBBY: There you go!

PATSY: But still, I fear he's capable of doing almost anything for money.

BOBBY: Why do some have so much and others so little? Is that just? So I am attempting to redress some wrongs, that's all.

MORGAN: (*to Patsy*) Thank you, Mr. Murphy. (*He sits down.*)

JUDGE: You are excused, Mr. Murphy.

BOBBY: Good-bye, old boy. No hard feelings. Until next time. You know, I've learned a few new tricks, so watch out!

(*Patsy bows and leaves to the right.*)

JUDGE: (*to Bailiff*) Call the next witness.

BAILIFF: Mr. Chickering Carter.

CHICK: Here!

(*He goes to the witness stand.*)

SAM: (*low to Jim*) Watch it! Catherine gave me the signal.

JUDGE: (*to Chick*) You swear to tell the truth, all the truth and nothing but the truth?

(*Chick places his hand on the Bible held out to him by the Bailiff.*)

CHICK: I do.

D.A.: (*to Chick*) Would you tell us your name and profession?

CHICK: Chickering Carter, private detective, working in the employ of Mr. Nick Carter, my boss.

D.A.: You were present at the attempted kidnapping of Miss Dodler on the night of January 14?

CHICK: Yes, sir.

D.A.: What was your role in the affair?

CHICK: I had to struggle with two ruffians that Melvil and Bobby had brought along to stand watch. I eventually won, but they managed to escape and I was unable to arrest them.

BOBBY: They'll be found!

CHICK: I hope so.

(*Melvil and Bobby lean forward, their elbows on the table, hiding their heads in their hands.*)

D.A. (*to Morgan*): Do you have any questions for this witness?

MORGAN: None.

JUDGE: (*to Chick*) You are excused.

(*Chick bows and leaves to the right.*)

JUDGE: (*to the D.A.*) Do you have any more witnesses?

D.A.: Only one, Your Honor.

JUDGE: Bailiff, call the last witness.

BAILIFF: Mr. Arizona Jack.

ARIZONA JACK: Whoop!

(*Jack goes to the witness stand.*)

JUDGE: What kind of noise was that?

ARIZONA JACK: The war cry of the cowboys of Arizona, Your Honor.

JUDGE: As we're not at war here, and not in Arizona either, don't injure our ears! Do you swear to tell the truth, all the truth and nothing but the truth?

ARIZONA JACK: I never lie, Your Honor. Let me swallow my head if I don't tell the truth.

BAILIFF: (*presenting the Bible to him*) Swear on the Bible.

ARIZONA JACK: I do.

D.A.: Would you tell us your name and profession?

ARIZONA JACK: William Hereford Theodore Benjamin–but my friends call me Arizona Jack–cowboy from Tucson, Arizona. Whoop!

JUDGE: (*severely*) See here!

ARIZONA JACK: Beg your pardon, Your Honor! Force of habit. I came to New York to have a splash and spend my money! I made the acquaintance of the great Nick Carter in a brawl in which he saved my life. From that time on, I've belonged to him, body and soul, from tip to toe.

D.A.: Tell us what you know about Miss Dodler's attempted kidnapping?

ARIZONA JACK: I knocked out the driver of their coach.

D.A.: Is that all?

ARIZONA JACK: The driver thought it was enough.

(*At this moment, Catherine, seated at the back, lets out a terrible, piercing scream.*)

CATHERINE: Aaaaah! Help! Help me! Aaaaah!

VARIOUS: What's the matter? What's going on? It's a woman! She's ill!

CATHERINE: (*screaming louder*) Help me! I'm dying! Help! I'm choking!

(*Great disturbance in the courtroom. People stand on chairs and benches. The public invades the area reserved for the witnesses, shouting and elbowing each other. The D.A. tries to figure out what's going on. The*

Judge coughs and bangs his gavel, but in vain. Catherine continues to shout. The uproar grows more intense. Davis, Morgan and the journalists stand up, thus hiding Melvil and Bobby from sight. Then, Jim and Sam get up, put on their overcoats, slink through the crowd and discreetly replace Melvil and Bobby, who sneak out to the right, without being noticed. Finally, the Sergeant-at-Arms reaches Catherine, still screaming, and removes her–they, too, leave out to the right. Calm is reestablished. Everybody resumes his place. Jim and Sam are dressed exactly like Melvil and Bobby, whom they resemble as much as possible, and are seated with their heads in their hands. The D.A. resumes his place.)

D.A.: It was an epileptic woman who's just been taken away. (*To Arizona Jack*) Do you recognize the two accused, here present?

ARIZONA JACK (*surprised*): Why, no, I don't recognize them at all. It's not them! They're gone!

(*Commotion in the courtroom.*)

D.A.: What?

(*Jim and Sam look at him sneeringly.*)

JUDGE: For goodness' sake!

ARIZONA JACK: I'll eat my head if these two scumbags don't resemble the other two, though.

D.A.: (*furious, to the Police*) Officers! Lock up these two! (*Pointing to Jim and Sam.*) And start looking for the prisoners! I want a full report in the hour!

MESSENGER: (*entering from the right*) A message for Mr. Morgan.

MORGAN: Here!

(*Morgan takes the letter and the messenger leaves.*)

JUDGE: What is it?

MORGAN: A note from my client, Your Honor. From Mr. Paddock. (*He reads:*) "To cure a cold, boil a pound of potatoes with ten ounces of onions–and take a powder. Serve hot. Pirithous."

(*Laughter.*)

JUDGE: (*furious*) This session is over!

(*The Judge leaves by the left, furious.*)

ARIZONA JACK: Whoop!

(*The D.A. points to Jim and Sam, who are led off by three Policemen despite mimed protests by their lawyers.*)

CURTAIN

ACT II

Scene II. Melvil's apartment

The furniture is banal. To the right, there is a fireplace, and to its right, a door in a cutaway. Center stage are a couch, at an angle, and a table. To the left, there is a window, also in a cutaway, and another door. There is a third door at the back. All three doors are masked by curtains.

Bobby Paddock, on his knees, finishes painting a large sign balanced on two chairs reading "Room to Rent."

BOBBY: (*singing*) From the moment that I told you
           Count on me, Josephine.
           To eat in the kitchen with you.
           But I don't like kippered herring
           I like veal barbecues.
           If you want me to adore you
           Gimme cod!

(*Catherine enters from the right carrying a bottle and two small glasses. She speaks in an affected, snooty way.*)

CATHERINE: Still the same song on your lips, Mr. Paddock?

50

BOBBY: (*rising and admiring his work*) Always, my pretty Catherine! (*Pointing to the sign.*) Take a look at that for me! Is it fine or what? If the Boss isn't pleased–

CATHERINE: Mr. Melvil hasn't come back?

BOBBY: Not yet, no. (*Pointing to the bottle.*) What's that that you're bringing us?

CATHERINE: (*filling glasses*) Rum.

BOBBY: Honest? (*He drinks and smacks his lips.*) Yes, famous. It's like sucking from an old slipper.

CATHERINE (*after having drunk herself*) That's the way to ruin your health, Mr. Paddock.

BOBBY: Yes, my Katey. (*Emptying his glass.*) That's the way to do it.

CATHERINE: Truly, men are not reasonable. (*Emptying her glass.*)

(*Jim and Sam enter from the right.*)

JIM: It's us!

SAM: Here we are!

CATHERINE: Ah, Jim, Sam!

BOBBY: (*shaking their hands*) They let you go?

SAM: An hour ago.

JIM: A week in the can–not much of a treat, eh?

BOBBY: But it was really worth it. We slipped through their fingers like butter!

SAM: While our wonderful Catherine was screeching like a polecat.

CATHERINE: (*screaming as before*) Help me! I'm dying! Help! I'm choking!

(*All four double up in laughter.*)

SAM: If only you'd seen the mug of the D. A. when he saw us!

JIM: And what about the Judge? He was foaming!

(*More laughter.*)

BOBBY: Two more glasses, Catherine.

CATHERINE: Right away, Mr. Paddock.

(*She leaves by the right.*)

JIM: Nothing new here during the last week?

BOBBY: No, nothing! Complete calm! But you've got here just in time: we're going back to work soon. (*They start smoking.*)

SAM: Ah! A good piece of business?

BOBBY: I really don't know. But I think it's got to do with the Dodler gal again! The Boss wants her, that kid! He intends to have her at all costs.

JIM: Well, she *is* pretty.

SAM: He's really nuts about her?

BOBBY: My word– that's what I'm asking myself! Is he after the money or the girl? No good to say that to him. You know how he doesn't like telling his business much.

(*Catherine returns with two more glasses. She pours rum in all four glasses; they all drink and talk.*)

BOBBY: What I'm afraid of is that he might do some dumb things.

JIM: What dumb things?

BOBBY: Well, this Dodler gal–Nick Carter is still watching over her like a hawk!

SAM: Damn!

BOBBY: And if the Boss is really infatuated with her– that could lead him astray, and consequently, us too.

JIM: Damn women! May the Devil take them!

BOBBY: Yes–love is bad for business.

CATHERINE: (*soulfully*) Oh, don't speak ill of love, Mr. Paddock.

BOBBY: (*mocking her*) No, my sweetie.

SAM: But what makes you think that Mr. Melvil isn't just after her money?

BOBBY: I repeat: I know nothing for sure, but I observe! Well–he's no longer the same; he's grown distracted; he sighs; he talks to himself–what's more, he no longer drinks. And to me, when a man reaches that point, he's cooked! And then, he spends all his time at the Red House, that old castle that he bought, an hour from New York. He's rebuilding it. He's added every defense possible there; he intends to turn it into a fortress. "When this is finished," he said to me, "they won't be able to get in here, except with a cannon."

JIM: Holy cow!

BOBBY: He's just booby-trapped it with electricity. If you touch the doorbell, a key, a window– BANG!

CATHERINE: It explodes?

BOBBY: You get a lightning bolt through your body.

CATHERINE: Lord!

BOBBY: My guess is that he intends to hide the lass at the Red House after he's got his hooks into her–which won't be long.

JIM: Ah?

BOBBY: Yes, this very day–in two hours–the pretty Helen Dodler will be his! He's designed a new scheme–it's a jewel! Ah, my friends, if the beauty escapes him this time, I won't drink anything but water for the rest of this week.

SAM: The Boss is going to come here?

BOBBY: I'm expecting him. And, by the way, before I forget, Sam, help me carry the other end.

(*Bobby and Sam pick up the freshly-painted sign.*)

JIM: (*reading*) "Furnished apartment to rent."

BOBBY: We're going to hang it on the balcony.

(*He opens the window and puts the sign outside.*)

JIM: Is the Boss moving?

BOBBY: I don't know. He told me to make a sign, I make a sign.

SAM: Speaking of the Dodler gal, if the Boss really has ideas about her, he'd better beware of Carmen.

JIM: Yeah! That would be prudent! Now here's one woman who can't take a joke.

BOBBY: But what a beautiful girl!

JIM: Oh–superb. But very jealous!

BOBBY: Yes, she adores Mr. Melvil, and I wouldn't give a dime for the skin of any rival of hers.

JIM: Where is Carmen?

BOBBY: In France, for the last two months, entrusted with an important mission.

SAM: I guess Mr. Melvil's going to be busy! Carmen on one side, Nick Carter on the other.

BOBBY: Oh, that Nick Carter, he'd better watch out! If he falls into our clutches, that bird, all he'll be is a snack.

JIM: The annoying thing is, when he turns up, everything goes wrong.

(*Carmen enters from the left, dressed in a travel outfit.*)

CARMEN: Hello, everybody.

(*The others are stupefied.*)

CARMEN: Everything's OK here?

BOBBY: Carmen!

JIM: Ah, for goodness' sake!

CARMEN: What's the matter with you? Do I frighten you?

BOBBY: We didn't expect to see you.

CATHERINE: You weren't supposed to be back for another week yet. What's going on?

CARMEN: (*smiling*) I changed my mind. Is Melvil here?

BOBBY: No, he's not.

CARMEN: Is he well?

BOBBY: In superb health.

CARMEN: Where is he?

BOBBY: Ah–that, I don't know.

CARMEN: How's business?

BOBBY: So-so.

CARMEN: Nothing special happened during my absence?

BOBBY: No, nothing.

SAM: Well, yes, we just spent a week in jail.

CARMEN: Bah! You got out! Why were you there?

BOBBY: (*signaling Sam to shut-up*) A robbery went wrong. They stupidly allowed themselves to be caught.

CARMEN: (*smiling*) That's shameful! To let yourself get pinched by the cops at your age! (*To Catherine*) Get me some hot water and have my trunks brought to my room.

CATHERINE: Right away, Miss Carmen.

(*She leaves by the right.*)

CARMEN: Ah, I'm really happy to be back.

(*She leaves by the back.*)

BOBBY: (*to Sam*) Can't you hold your tongue, you idiot!

SAM: What? What did I say?

BOBBY: If I hadn't stopped you, you were going to tell her about the kidnapping, the Boss's arrest, the trial, the whole story.

SAM: So?

BOBBY: What if the Boss doesn't want Carmen to know about it?

JIM: Which is likely.

SAM: She'll find out sooner or later.

BOBBY: Possibly! But don't let it be from you, that's my advice, and it's good advice. He might make you pay for it, idiot.

JIM: The Boss is brutal.

(*Suddenly, Melvil rushes in from the right; he wears a wig and fake mustache; he goes to the window and looks out cautiously.*)

BOBBY: (*low*) Here he is!

MELVIL: Come here, Bobby, and look. (*Bobby goes to the window.*) Careful! Don't be seen. What do you see?

BOBBY: A thousand devils! Nick Carter!

MELVIL: Ah! He noticed the sign!

BOBBY: He's leaving.

MELVIL: Not for long. (*To Jim and Sam.*) Ah, here you are, my brave fellows? They released you?

JIM: An hour ago.

MELVIL: You were both superb the other day. I'm pleased with you. (*He gives them each a banknote.*) Here–twenty dollars. (*He removes his hat and coat.*) You come just in the nick of time. I have need of you. Go to Meltcraft's Tavern in Chatham Square–

JIM: The Rat Trap?

MELVIL: Yes, the Rat Trap. Tell Meltcraft to fix up a room right away.

JIM: Yes, Boss.

MELVIL: Then wait for me at the bar. Go! Quick! And leave by the cellar. There are probably cops in the street.

(*Jim and Sam leave quickly by the right.*)

BOBBY: So Nick Carter has followed you.

MELVIL: Yes, he's fallen into my trap, the fool! Only he could cause my plan to fail now. Therefore, we must isolate him at all costs.

BOBBY: Is that why you're disguised?

MELVIL: Purposefully so. In such a way that I knew he would easily recognize me. Earlier, I took a stroll on Mulberry Street, across from the Police Headquarters. Nick Carter goes there almost every day to chat and smoke a cigar with the Chief Inspector. I strolled up and down for around 20 minutes. When Carter left, he saw me and set out to follow me, doing his best to remain hidden. Ah, I made that animal run, I'll answer for that. For a good hour and a half, I dragged him in tow, sometimes on foot, sometimes on the tramway, pretending all the while not to see him. Finally, I led him here and I came in, leaving him on the sidewalk from where he could see the "Room for Rent" sign.

BOBBY: You took a big risk. Suppose he'd arrested you–

MELVIL: I wasn't in any danger! First of all, I had my eye on him and I wouldn't let myself be taken easily. Besides, I knew he really wants to know where I live, to catch us in a dragnet.

BOBBY: You think that he's going to return?

MELVIL: Without the shadow of a doubt. I'm going to tell Catherine. (*He heads to the right.*)

BOBBY: (*lowering his voice*) No, wait.

MELVIL: What is it?

BOBBY: Carmen's here.

MELVIL: (*speechless*) Carmen! It can't be!

BOBBY: She just arrived. (*pointing to the back*) She's there–in her room.

MELVIL: The Devil! (*furious*) Why did she return early?

BOBBY: I don't know.

MELVIL: Someone betrayed me? Warned her?

BOBBY: I don't think so. She seems very happy and doesn't appear to suspect anything.

MELVIL: (*enraged*) To be so close to success, to reach my goal, and now this wretched thing, which might wreck all my plans! Does she know about my arrest, my trial?

BOBBY: No, she didn't say a word about it.

MELVIL: Let her beware! If she works against me, or if she touches a single hair of the one I love–

BOBBY: (*timidly*) Miss Helen?

MELVIL: (*roughly*) Shut up! (*short silence*) Well, yes, I love her, I adore her, I'm mad about her–

BOBBY: (*aside*) Now, that's what I was afraid of.

MELVIL: The day I saw her, Bobby, everything changed for me.

BOBBY: So I've noticed.

MELVIL: She's my whole life; I only think of her! Me, Fantômas! Melvil! The King of Crime! A young girl holds me in her hand, her gaze troubles me, her grace conquers me, her voice makes me tremble, and I would kill myself, yes, kill myself, here, right now, without hesitation, if I were sure that she would never love me.

BOBBY: (*aside*) Ah, the power of women! Here we are in a fine mess.

MELVIL: (*getting control of himself*) We mustn't lose our heads...

BOBBY: No, now is not the time!

MELVIL: Nothing is lost yet! With a cool head, some audacity–

BOBBY: Right.

MELVIL: –I will find a way.

BOBBY: By Jove, you've never lacked ideas before.

MELVIL: (*looking out the window, then returning*) But above all, we must get rid of Nick Carter.

BOBBY: Yes, that's the important thing!

MELVIL: If he no longer stood in our way–

BOBBY: That would indeed make things easier.

MELVIL: With a bloke of that sort, one must be careful. So when he enters, you will hide there, behind this curtain. (*He points to the left*.)

BOBBY: Understood.

(*Carmen enters, now dressed in town clothes*.)

CARMEN: (*she embraces Melvil passionately*) Finally, you're back, my darling!

MELVIL: (*pretending astonishment*) Ah! For goodness' sake! Carmen! My Carmen! You're back?

CARMEN: You didn't know? Bobby didn't tell you?

BOBBY: My word, no! I plain forgot about it. The Boss was telling me some serious things.

CARMEN: What things?

BOBBY: Nick Carter's going to come here.

CARMEN: (*terrified*) Great God! Here?

MELVIL: Very soon.

CARMEN: Quick–get away!

MELVIL: No–I'm in no danger. I'm the one who lured him here.

CARMEN: I don't understand.

MELVIL: I've set a trap for him! I'll explain everything
to you later. (*To Bobby.*) Watch at the window and take care that no one sees you.

(*Bobby does as ordered.*)

CARMEN: Ah, my darling, my love! How I longed to
get back! I was dying without you!

MELVIL: Really?

CARMEN: Ah, yes! Two long months so far from you!
So very far!

MELVIL: I wrote you often.

CARMEN: What are letters? And they were so cold, so
indifferent! You haven't cheated on me, at
least?

BOBBY: (*aside*) Not for lack of trying!

MELVIL: (*indignant*) Oh, Carmen, Carmen, how can
you think such a thing even for a moment?

CARMEN: Swear to me that you don't love another
woman!

MELVIL: Me!

CARMEN: That idea wouldn't leave me; it gnawed at
me–

MELVIL: You're crazy! How could I no longer love you–

BOBBY: (*aside*) He has cheek!

CARMEN: It's because of that I came back earlier. To catch you, to surprise you!

BOBBY: (*aside*) She's got a nose!

CARMEN: Swear to me that you don't love another woman! Swear!

MELVIL: Why, of course–as often as you like.

BOBBY: (*aside*) For what that costs him!

CARMEN: I love you so very much! (*She kisses him.*) I've got you under my skin, in my heart, in my blood.

BOBBY: (*aside*) Everywhere, except her head!

MELVIL: Dearest Carmen! Tell me: did you succeed in Normandy?

CARMEN: Completely. Three days after my arrival, I made the acquaintance of Harry Pelham–a nice man, you know! A week later, we were the best friends in the world.

MELVIL: In all good honor, I hope, eh?

CARMEN: Darling! He's 70!

MELVIL: I'm always wary of rich old men (*Bobby laughs*.) What did you learn about him?

CARMEN: First of all, as you said, he's indeed rich.

MELVIL: Good!

CARMEN: He has no children, he never married, and he plans to leave his entire fortune to his god-daughter, a Miss Helen Dodler, who lives in New York.

MELVIL: What's he like physically?

CARMEN: A fine and tall old man, who still has all his hair–cut short, with a fine white beard. I brought you a photograph.

MELVIL: Excellent!

CARMEN: He's coming here very soon to attend the wedding of this Miss Helen, whom he loves deeply. She was nine when he left–

BOBBY: Watch out! I think Carter's coming!

MELVIL: (*rushing to the window, followed by Carmen*) Yes, that's him.

CARMEN: You're sure?

MELVIL: Absolutely! He's coming here. (*To Carmen.*)

Quick, go open the door for him. He'll ask to visit the furnished apartment. Take him here, then go to your room. (*The doorbell rings.*) He's ringing the bell!

CARMEN: Are you going to kill him?

MELVIL: (*pushing her*) Get going!

(*Carmen leaves rapidly by the right.*)

BOBBY: You've got your revolver, Boss?

MELVIL: Yes, don't worry. What are you doing?

BOBBY: I'm taking off my boots. You don't know. It might be useful.

MELVIL: (*pointing to the curtain at the left*) Hide!

BOBBY: Right! Right!

(*Bobby takes his boots in his hand and hides behind the curtained door.*)

MELVIL: And be careful to not let him suspect your presence! (*Thinking.*) Let's see. I'll need some rope. (*He takes a coil of rope out of a drawer and puts it in his pocket.*) Ah! And cigars, too. Those nice cigars that cause sleep! (*He takes a box of cigars, places them on the table near which he sits, pretending to read a newspaper.*)

(*Nick Carter, disguised as an old man, enters.*)

CARMEN: Come in, sir, I beg you. My husband will answer all your questions.

(*Carmen bows and leaves by the back.*)

MELVIL: (*turning*) Who is it?

NICK: I'm Mister Jones.

MELVIL: (*rising*) Oh! Excuse me, sir! I beg you to forgive me, I was reading the newspaper! An exciting affair!

NICK: The papers are full of exciting affairs and have been for a long while.

MELVIL: Indeed! Indeed! What can I do for you, Mister Jones?

NICK: Oh, a small thing.

MELVIL: Would you be seated?

NICK: No, thanks. I'm not tired. (*They are face to face and look each other carefully in the eyes.*) I understand that you have a furnished apartment to let?

MELVIL: This is it.

NICK: Ah! How soon will it be free?

MELVIL: In a week.

NICK: How many rooms?

MELVIL: Five. A salon, a dining room, two bedrooms and a kitchen.

NICK: That's just what I need.

MELVIL: In that case, please sit down.

NICK: No, truly, I assure you, I prefer to stand. But if you yourself would like to sit down–

MELVIL: No, I, too, prefer to remain standing.

NICK: Then neither of us will sit. (*laughing*)

MELVIL: (*laughing*) Neither of us, right. A cigar? (*presenting the box.*)

NICK: No, thanks.

MELVIL: They are excellent.

NICK: I don't smoke. But don't bother about me. I don't find smoke at all unpleasant.

MELVIL: No, I no longer smoke.

NICK: Is the place quiet? Because, I'm telling you, I insist on absolute peace and–

MELVIL: Oh, it's more than quiet.

NICK: No cats? No dogs? No piano? No children? I absolutely insist.

(*Suddenly, Melvil leaps on Carter and takes him by the
throat, seeking to strangle him. The two men roll on the
ground. Nick gets loose and pummels his foe. There is a
fierce and mostly silent struggle. After several minutes,
Nick has Melvil on the ground, held under his knee. At
this moment, Bobby emerges from behind the curtain
with a club in his hand. He strikes Nick, who lets out a
yell and rolls over, unconscious. Carmen appears at the
back.*)

CARMEN: Well?

BOBBY: It's all over!

MELVIL: The Devil! Just in time! The scoundrel was
strangling me.

BOBBY: I saw that.

MELVIL: What a punch!

CARMEN: Is he dead?

MELVIL: (*leaning over Nick*) No, his heart is still beating.

BOBBY: (*brandishing his club*) Then I'll finish him off.

MELVIL: No! Not now! Take this rope (*He hands him
the rope.*) and tie him up. We'll kill him tonight and then, get rid of the body.

(*Bobby takes the rope and they tie Nick up as they chat.*)

BOBBY: Jolly good!

MELVIL: Right now, we're pressed for time. We don't have a moment to lose. They're waiting for us!

CARMEN: Where?

MELVIL: At Meltcraft's.

CARMEN: Is it part of your plan?

MELVIL: Yes. And it's a good one.

CARMEN: Am I going with you?

MELVIL: No–you stay here!

CARMEN: Why?

MELVIL: It's necessary; I need you here. You'll be watching Carter–don't leave him alone, even for a second. You have your gun?

CARMEN: It's in my room.

MELVIL: Go get it.

(*Carmen goes out by the rear.*)

BOBBY: (*lowering his voice*) Great idea! That way, she won't be bothering us!

MELVIL: That's why I prevented you from killing him.

BOBBY: I see now.

MELVIL: Grab him by the feet–(*gloating*) Nick Carter, King of Detectives!

(*Melvil takes Carter by the shoulders, Bobby grabs his feet. They carry the Detective to the sofa, so that his head is supported by the headboard.*)

BOBBY: (*to Nick, still unconscious*) Well, old friend, not feeling so good, right now? Some trouble with your heart perhaps? That's what you get for meddling in things that don't concern you! I'd give you something to read to pass the time, but as your eyes are still shut, it's not worth the bother.

MELVIL: (*putting on his coat and hat*) Go to Melt-craft's to pick up Jim and Sam and bring them back with you. It's 3:30 p.m. Miss Dodler won't visit her new residence until 5 p.m.

BOBBY: Yes, we've got plenty of time.

(*Nick Carter opens his eyes and shuts them quickly.*)

CARMEN: (*returning, revolver in hand.*) OK!

MELVIL: It's understood? You won't leave him, under any pretext?

CARMEN: Don't worry.

MELVIL: If he budges, knock him on the head.

CARMEN: Count on me.

(*Carmen places her revolver on the table.*)

MELVIL: On our way, Bobby.

BOBBY: (*putting on his boots.*) Coming! Coming!

MELVIL: (*to Carmen*) And do not open to anyone! You understand? Anyone!

CARMEN: (*embracing Melvil*) Return soon, my darling.

MELVIL: As quickly as possible, I promise you. Goodbye! (*aside*) Whew! (*aloud*) Let's go, Bobby.

BOBBY: Coming, coming.

(*Melvil and Bobby leave by the right. Carmen looks at Nick: he still appears to be unconscious. She shrugs and then goes out by the back.*)

NICK: (*quietly opening his eyes*) Lucky break I decided to wear a padded wig. A bit heavy, not too elegant perhaps, but so precious! (*A pause.*) Am I going to remain alone? (*Another pause.*) Poor little Helen, she doesn't suspect the danger that threatens her. If Patsy and Chick are not watching over her, it's all over,

she's lost. (*Third pause.*) They've tied me up
like a roast of beef, the brutes, and so tight–

(*Suddenly, he shuts his eyes as Carmen returns, holding
a shirt which she sets to mending, seated at the table.*)

CARMEN: It's going to be fun to stay alone with this
imbecile.

NICK: (*aside*) Thanks.

CARMEN: And I was hoping that he wasn't going to
leave me for the whole day.

NICK: (*aside*) The lady is in love with Melvil.

CARMEN: (*sings*) Love is a gypsy child,
It has never, never, known a law;
Love me not, then I love you;
If I love you, you'd best beware! [2]

NICK: (*in a weak voice*) Bravo!

CARMEN: (*looking at him*) Heavens! So you've come
to?

NICK: Almost!

CARMEN: At last. Are you feeling better?

NICK: Ouch! Not so much!

---

[2] From the opera *Carmen* by Georges Bizet.

CARMEN: What a crazy idea to come charging after folks in their own home! You really are not reasonable, Mr. Carter.

NICK: Alas, Miss, I see that plainly now! Still, I don't feel too bad. I was lucky in my misfortune: they could have killed me, and I'm still alive. I could be watched by some frightful rogue, but instead I'm watched by a woman–a beautiful, ravishing woman.

CARMEN: (*still sewing*) Oh! My, you're quite gallant!

NICK: I adore women, it's true. Would you do me a great favor?

CARMEN: Alas, my dear Mr. Carter, I can't. All I can do for you is break your head with this gun if you budge an inch! That's an order!

NICK: Me, budge! How could I? I can't move–either my feet or my hands. No, what I was going to ask of you was for you to turn towards me so I can see your pretty face. That will cost you no great effort, and my eyes will be delighted by it.

CARMEN: Is that all it takes to be agreeable to you? (*She turns and resumes sewing.*)

NICK: Nothing else, thanks! This way, I'm not going to be bored for a single moment. There's nothing more captivating than the face of a beautiful woman.

CARMEN: You're nice, Mr. Carter, but I am not completely stupid. You want to soften me up, wheedle me, cajole me.

NICK: Oh, not at all! I won't speak to you if it displeases you. I will content myself with gazing at you. Your neck is delightful; your nose is adorable.

CARMEN: (*laughing*) You *are* funny! You do know that they're going to kill you tonight?

NICK: (*very calm*) Come on, that's impossible. Before dinner?

CARMEN: No, after.

NICK: Ah! For a moment, you scared me!

CARMEN: That all it does to you?

NICK: By Jove! I'm used to it! Each morning, when I get up, I tell myself that I probably won't see the end of the day. And that thought doesn't disturb me in the least.

CARMEN: Ah, you are brave.

NICK: Indifferent, rather. If I told you that I fear death less than a head cold–

CARMEN: (*laughing*) Ah! For goodness' sake!

NICK: To cough, sniffle, spit, wipe one's nose, with swollen eyes, is intolerable torture for me.

CARMEN: (*still laughing*) You are amusing!

NICK: Ah! Laugh some more, I beg you! You have the prettiest mouth in the world.

CARMEN: No, truly, you amaze me.

NICK: Why?

CARMEN: You're joking when—

NICK: No, not at all! I'm not joking. Your mouth is exquisite.

CARMEN: Still, you have no more than a few hours to live and—

NICK: You are embellishing them! What more could I wish for? I assure you that, but for my head which still hurts a little, and these ropes that bind me a bit too tight, this afternoon seems most pleasant to me!

CARMEN: You're not very difficult!

NICK: Life is so boring.

CARMEN: You're bored?

NICK: Ah, yes! I suffer from neurasthenia!

CARMEN: I would have thought that, in your business–

NICK: On the contrary, even there, there are so few surprises! Which is why I welcome anything that comes and disturb my routine. For example, right now, if I wasn't stupidly hogtied and helpless, I'd be rushing to the rescue of a young girl whom Mr. Melvil has sworn to kidnap and whom I have sworn to protect.

CARMEN: (*excitedly*) A young girl?

NICK: A stunningly beautiful girl, with whom he's passionately in love.

CARMEN: You're crazy.

(*Carmen rises and begins to pace.*)

NICK: Me? I'm telling the truth. As a matter of fact, he's already tried to kidnap her once before.

CARMEN: (*stops short*) Once before?

NICK: Yes. His first attempt didn't succeed because I was there. I was on watch and lucky enough to be able to snatch his victim from him.

CARMEN: (*beside herself*) When was that?

NICK: About a month ago. I arrested Melvil and Bobby, who were tried a week ago, but managed to escape right in the midst of the hearing. You haven't heard about it?

CARMEN: (*with growing fury*) Bobby, too, eh? No! I knew nothing! I wasn't here. I was in France, where he'd sent me. To get rid of me, no doubt!

NICK: I see.

CARMEN: And he's planning to kidnap that girl again today?

NICK: In an hour, yes. This time, after having taken care to remove me from his path. Ah, poor Miss Dodler! She's lost, I fear, quite lost.

CARMEN: (*surprised*) Miss Dodler, you say! Her name wouldn't be Helen Dodler?

NICK: Why, yes! Do you know her?

CARMEN: Ah, this is too much! How dare he! Harry Pelham's goddaughter!

NICK: You know Mr. Pelham, too?

CARMEN: Ah, the wretch! He'll pay for this!

NICK: Who, Melvil? I don't think you're likely to see him again.

CARMEN: Really?

NICK: It would surprise me greatly if he were to bring his new conquest here.

CARMEN: Jesus! He's going to take her to the Red House.

NICK: The Red House?

CARMEN: (*training her revolver on Nick*) Where is Melvil at this moment? Tell me! Where is the place of this kidnapping?

NICK: I'm not going to tell you.

CARMEN: In that case, I'll be the one to kill you.

NICK: What will that get you? You know nothing. And if I haven't reappeared in a quarter of an hour, the police will storm this house. No, there's only one way for you to stop Melvil– only one way!

CARMEN: Which is?

NICK: Let's both go!

CARMEN: Both of us! Me, with you?

NICK: That's my only condition. And so we don't waste a minute, we'll take my automobile.

CARMEN: So be it! (*threateningly*) But if you lied to me...

(*She goes out by the back.*)

NICK: (*alone*) See, one must never despair! Isn't life a thrill, with its surprises and twists of luck! And to think there are folks who are bored!

(*Carmen returns with her hat and coat.*)

CARMEN: Come on, quick!

NICK: Gladly, but–

CARMEN: Wait! (*she cuts his bonds with a dagger.*)

NICK: Ah, that feels much better. (*He removes his wig.*) Aie! I must have a bump as big as an egg! Well, no matter. Let's get going!

CARMEN: You know, Carter, if you've made a fool of me, if you've deceived me, I will kill you.

NICK: Of course! Let's get moving, my dear Carmen!

(*They go out to the right.*)

CURTAIN

Scene III. George Clancy's house

A large, luxurious room that has not been fully furnished. Several boxes, as yet unpacked, and pictures are on the floor, leaning against the wall. In the back, a large door opens on a winter garden filled with plants and flowers. There are other doors near the audience and in the cutaway.

Two Upholsterers, standing on ladders, are installing curtain holders over the door in the cutaway at the left. Deborah enters from the right, carrying a tablecloth and three tea servings. She's an old woman wearing a bonnet that covers a wig. Its false hair forms two grey bands framing her face.

DEBORAH: (to the Upholsters) Well, are you asleep? You haven't yet finished installing the rods?

FIRST UPHOLSTERER: We need time.

DEBORAH: Ah, you are certainly taking it! It's plain to see you are paid by the hour!

(George Clancy and Patsy Murphy enter by the right cutaway. George is dressed in the uniform of a Navy Lieutenant.)

83

GEORGE: Hello, Deborah!

DEBORAH: Ah, Mr. Clancy! You surprised me. I wasn't expecting you.

GEORGE: (*smiling*) One can't be too careful!

PATSY: Hush! Wait! (*He goes to look at the Upholsterers.*) No, no danger. They're real curtain-hangers.

GEORGE: You had a doubt?

PATSY: Not really, but my instructions are clear. Until you're married to Miss Dodler, I'm responsible for you.

DEBORAH: (*recognizing him*) Why, it's Mr. Murphy!

PATSY: Hush! For the moment, Miss Deborah, I'm the valiant Commodore Palmer.

GEORGE: My captain and my friend on leave in New York, who has come to greet my fiancée.

PATSY: Don't you forget it!

DEBORAH: Commodore Palmer? Right! Don't worry, it's understood.

(*She prepares tea at the back right.*)

PATSY: No one has come since this morning?

DEBORAH: No one, except these two workmen whom I
know.

(*The Upholsterers come down from their ladder.*)

FIRST UPHOLSTERER: There, it's finished.

DEBORAH: At last! Well, remove the scaffolding!

SECOND UPHOLSTERER: With pleasure, Miss Deborah. (*aside*) Old bag!

GEORGE: Here, my dear chaps. (*He gives them a tip.*)

FIRST UPHOLSTERER: Thank you, sir! (*aside*) At
least, a good man.

(*The Upholsterers leave by the right.*)

PATSY: (*to George*) Tell me, how many keys open the
entrance door to this mansion?

GEORGE: Four. I have one.

DEBORAH: Me, too.

GEORGE: And I gave the other two keys to Nick Carter
and Miss Helen.

PATSY: Fine!

DEBORAH: Don't worry, Mr. Murph–(*catching herself*)
Commodore. No one can get in here without

my permission. You can rely on me. I've got a good eye.

PATSY: I have the utmost confidence in you, Miss Deborah, but that still won't stop me from inspecting every nook and cranny of this house, from the cellars below right up to the roof above. That's Mr. Carter's order. I'm now going to make my rounds.

(*Patsy leaves by the right.*)

DEBORAH: How beautiful it is here today.

GEORGE: Once we're settled in and our furniture has arrived, I hope the house will please Helen.

DEBORAH: She hasn't seen it yet?

GEORGE: No, she's coming here today for the first time. She's impatient to see our future lodgings.

(*Ringing.*)

DEBORAH: Someone's at the door.

(*Deborah goes out to the right.*)

GEORGE: (*aside*) It's probably Helen, or Nick Carter. No, they both have keys.

DEBORAH: (*off*) This way.

(*She returns.*)

DEBORAH: They're bringing a piano; it would appear it's been shipped from France.

GEORGE: From France?

(*Jim and Sam, dressed like workmen, enter by the right, carrying a very large piano crate made of white wood, bearing various labels: Top-Bottom, Fragile, New York.*)

JIM: (*placing the box on the ground*) Jesus–

SAM: (*to Deborah*) Where do you want it, granny?

DEBORAH: (*upset*) I am not your grandmother, young man! Don't be rude!

SAM: (*laughing*) C'mon, don't get mad.

JIM: Where are we to put that thing?

GEORGE: (*pointing to the back right*) Here–against the wall.

JIM: (*to Sam*) Let's do it.

(*They pick up the crate and carry it to the spot indicated by George.*)

SAM: Are we supposed to open it?

DEBORAH: (*sharply*) Of course! I'm not going to un-pack a piano!

JIM: Easy, easy!

SAM: She doesn't seem very nice, does she?

JIM: We're going to make another delivery and return with our tools.

SAM: There'll be a tip in it, right? Because, you know, we don't have to unpack your piano.

GEORGE: You'll be happy, I promise you.

JIM: 'Til later. (*To Sam*) Very fancy, here.

SAM: Ah! It's better than our place.

DEBORAH: (*aside*) What a pair of scamps!

(*Jim and Sam leave, following Deborah, by the right.*)

GEORGE: (*reading a label nailed to the box*) This comes from Paris. From the Maison Erard! "Sent by Mr. Harry Pelham." Helen's godfather. It must be his wedding gift. Helen didn't tell me about it. A surprise, no doubt. She wasn't expecting it.

(*Deborah returns with cakes, liquors, glasses, etc and places them on the tea table.*)

GEORGE: It's Helen's godfather who's sent her a piano.

DEBORAH: Mr. Pelham?

GEORGE: Yes.

DEBORAH: Miss Helen is going to be very pleased. Ah, how nice the two of you will find things here.

(*Helen, her Aunt Margaret, Chick Carter and Arizona Jack enter by the right. Chick and Arizona Jack are dressed like upholsterers.*)

DEBORAH: (*to Helen*) Ah, there you are, dear.

HELEN: (*smiling*) Hello, Deborah! Hello, George darling!

GEORGE: Hello, Helen!

HELEN: Ah! It smells like paint in here. Open the window, please, Deborah.

(*Deborah opens the window.*)

GEORGE: (*bowing to Margaret*) Miss Margaret.

MARGARET: Ah, I was in a hurry to get here. My God, how afraid I was. We were followed.

CHICK: No, Miss, I swear to you that you're mistaken.

HELEN: (*laughing*) Look Auntie, you're not reasonable. (*to George*) Again, last night, she let out the most horrible screams.

MARGARET: I had a terrible nightmare.

HELEN: And as she sleeps beside me, to reassure me–or so she says–I woke up with a frightful start.

MARGARET: Ah, it was stronger than I was. Ever since I learned that that diabolical Mr. Melvil escaped, I live in dread! I see him everywhere. His gaze weighs on me. I'm afraid I'm going mad.

GEORGE: Come on, calm down.

HELEN: It's shameful to be a coward to this degree.

CHICK: No danger threatens you, Miss.

DEBORAH: (*to Helen*) Who are these workers?

HELEN: Two good friends, Mr. Chick Carter and Mr. Arizona Jack, disguised as curtain-hangers. The better to keep an eye on me.

CHICK: Order of Nick Carter.

HELEN: Where, then, is Mr. Carter?

MARGARET: Yes! We haven't seen him since last night.

CHICK: Further proof that you have nothing to worry about. (*To George*) Did Patsy come?

GEORGE: Yes.

CHICK: With the dogs?

GEORGE: Two fine animals which he left in the courtyard. Right now, he's inspecting the house.
From the cellars to the attic.

CHICK: (*to Arizona Jack*) We'll do the same. (*To Margaret*) Don't worry, Miss Margaret. You're
well guarded. Come on, Jack.

ARIZONA JACK: Whoop!

CHICK: Ah, no! Please, no whooping, huh?

(*The two leave by the right.*)

DEBORAH: As for me, I'm going to busy myself with
making the tea.

(*She leaves by the right.*)

HELEN: (*smiling*) Come on, collect yourself, Auntie.
You're safe here. There are three detectives
and two dogs to defend you. Isn't that
enough?

MARGARET: It's never too much! I don't have your
insane bravura!

HELEN: My goodness, you're not worthy of being the
daughter of pioneers!

GEORGE: (*pointing to the crate*) Come see what you've
got here. A piano. A piano from Erard!

HELEN: (*joyfully*) Truly?

GEORGE: And guess who sent it to you? Mr. Pelham.

HELEN: My godfather! Oh! How sweet of him!

MARGARET: How come he didn't mention it to you in the letter you received from him this morning?

HELEN: Because he wanted to surprise me.

GEORGE: He told you he's coming to the wedding?

HELEN: Yes, he sails the day after tomorrow on the *Touraine*... Can't we open this box? I'm in a hurry to see my piano.

GEORGE: The workmen who brought it went to get their tools. A bit of patience.

MARGARET: Well, I'm going to take a look around.

HELEN: Yes, that's an excellent idea. And don't hurry too much. Take your time.

MARGARET: You won't be bored?

HELEN: No, don't worry.

MARGARET: (*sighing*) Ah, how lucky she is!

(*Margaret leaves by the left. As soon as she has gone,*

George and Helen embrace.)

GEORGE: My dear love!

(*Patsy reappears at the right and discreetly disappears, so as not to bother the two fiancés*.)

HELEN: I always want to be with you, never to leave you.

GEORGE: In a week, you will be my wife.

HELEN: How long that week seems to me.

PATSY: (*entering, after first coughing discreetly*.) Hum!

HELEN: Oh! Someone! Who is this gentleman?

GEORGE: You don't recognize him?

PATSY: (*singing*) I was a Captain, I had a gay heart!

HELEN: Mr. Murphy!

PATSY: Himself!

GEORGE: Who made us spend such an interesting evening with his Irish songs!

PATSY: Really?

HELEN: For the last week, your melancholy refrain never left my mind. It's an obsession. (*singing*) I was a Captain, I had a gay heart...

PATSY: (*to George*) I've been through the house. I've seen everything, except the attic and the garret. Where are the service stairs?

GEORGE: (*pointing to the left*) Over that way. Through that room and the billiard room next to it.

PATSY: Thanks!

(*Patsy leaves by the left. Margaret returns from the rear.*)

HELEN: What, back already, Auntie?

MARGARET: Yes, all alone, I was too afraid! And besides, I'm really hungry! I'm going to tell Deborah to serve tea. I'm jealous, Helen. Have you seen the bathrooms?

HELEN: Why, no, I haven't seen the house at all.

MARGARET: Well, go see it! It's a marvel. George has made a folly.

HELEN: That doesn't surprise me! (*To George*) Offer me your arm, my prince charming, and do me the honors of your palace.

GEORGE: I'm entirely at your order, my princess.

(*George offers Helen his arm and leaves with her by the door at the left.*)

MARGARET: (*sighing*) How happy they are! Ah! Love, love! To say that I'll never know it! I'd give ten years of my life to be clasped to a male bosom, to be pressed tight, upset and trembling against a passionate heart. To feel myself carried off by two vigorous, manly arms.

(*Margaret has recited her rant in front of the crate, with her back to it. As she utters her last words, the front of the crate slides open silently. Melvil and Bobby, dressed just like Jim and Sam, emerge from inside the box. Melvil gags Margaret, Bobby ties her hands, and they lock her inside the crate.*)

BOBBY: One down! She won't bother us in there! This is much better. I was suffocating inside that crate.

MELVIL: You heard what they said?

BOBBY: And what they sang. I didn't miss a word.

MELVIL: Patsy is here.

BOBBY: As well as Chick and that idiot of a cowboy. (*imitating Arizona Jack*) Whoop!

MELVIL: Plus the Navy Lieutenant.

(*He goes to listen at the doors. Margaret can be heard kicking inside the crate.*)

BOBBY: (*opening the box*) Quiet down, you! No noise, my beautiful! (*He raps the box with his re-*

volver.) See that? It's my gun! If you make a racket, bang, I'll put a bullet in your coffee pot. (*He shuts the box.*)

MELVIL: Hush! Listen. They're coming.

(*They pretend to be busy with the case, as if they were intending to remove the nails. Deborah enters by the right, carrying a teapot with very hot tea.*)

DEBORAH: Here's the tea–it's boiling! (*She places the tea on the table.*) Nobody! (*She notices Melvil and Bobby, whose backs are turned toward her.*) What? You two are back? Who let you in? How did you get in? (*She walks toward them.*) Well, don't you hear me? Are you deaf, I am asking you–

(*Melvil and Bobby turn abruptly, grab her, tie her and gag her.*)

BOBBY: (*threatening her with his revolver*) No screaming, not a sound. (*He removes her bonnet and wig. She's almost bald.*) Oh, the poor woman. She's going to catch cold. (*He replaces her wig.*) Here, take it. It'll keep you warm. (*He threatens her with the gun.*) Now give us your skirt and your jacket.

(*Deborah gives her skirt and her jacket. They lock her inside the crate.*)

BOBBY: There's company in there already. You won't be bored.

(*Margaret tries to escape; they push her back.*)

BOBBY: The other one's trying the bolt now! Will you get back in there right away! Get back inside, or I'll break your leg! It's true what they say, women can't stay in one place. (*They shut the box.*) So much for the two of 'em! Business is brisk. (*He puts on Deborah's clothes and wig.*) What are you doing, Boss?

MELVIL: I'm pouring tea in two cups. And I've put a few drops in the third, so they'll think the aunt has already drunk hers.

BOBBY: Yes, not bad! That way, they won't be uneasy about her disappearance.

MELVIL: You've got your flask with the mixture?

BOBBY: Yes, all fresh. Here's my little bottle. It never leaves me.

MELVIL: Give it here.

BOBBY: (*giving Melvil a small bottle which he takes from his vest pocket*) It's so handy when you have the occasion to use it.

MELVIL: If only I knew which cup this imbecile Lieutenant would drink from...

BOBBY: You'd double the dose.

MELVIL: For sure.

BOBBY: (*listening to the left*) Hurry up! They're coming!

MELVIL: Go watch for the arrival of the automobile. Then let Jim and Sam in. With this disguise, you can move around the house without risk of being recognized. (*He opens the door on the left.*) As for me, I'll lock myself up in this room. You will warn me by rapping three times on the door. And no mistakes, get it? Now, let's get out of here fast.

(*Melvil leaves to the left. The bolt is heard.*)

BOBBY: Going fine, going fine!

(*Bobby rushes out to the right. George and Helen enter from the left.*)

GEORGE: It's true, you are hungry.

HELEN: Like a wolf! I'm going to tell Deborah to bring the tea.

GEORGE: Here it is, it's served.

HELEN: Well, to the table! (*They install themselves.*)

GEORGE (*after tasting the tea*) It's not very sweet.

HELEN: How much sugar. (*She takes a cube.*)

GEORGE: Just one.

HELEN: Three for me. I love sugar.

(*She puts one cube in George's cup and three in her own.*)

GEORGE: Little gourmand! (*sipping*) Yuck! It's dreadful.

HELEN: I have to have some faults, you wouldn't love me otherwise! Now where is my aunt? She was in such a hurry to have her cup of tea!

GEORGE: (*pointing to the third cup*) And she didn't wait for us! She's undoubtedly continuing her inspection of the house. And besides, she didn't want to bother us.

HELEN: (*after having drunk*) My word, I drank a whole cup. It's good.

GEORGE: A bit strong.

HELEN: No, I didn't think so.

GEORGE: And a peculiar taste.

HELEN: That, I found delicious! Are you busy with our marriage arrangements?

GEORGE: (*speaking slowly, with difficulty*) I'm... not busy... with it at all... Everything... is in order... The civil ceremony... the religious

ceremony... the banquet... the ball... everything. But our house... won't be ready–

HELEN: Oh, no!

GEORGE: ...So I've arranged... for a bridal suite... to be
booked at the Imperial Hotel. Fairylike deco-
rations... A profusion of lights and flowers...
Orchestra, choruses–you will be pleased...

HELEN: Don't forget a room for my godfather.

GEORGE: Right (*he dozes off.*)

HELEN: On the ground floor... if possible... he mentioned it to me... in his letter... (*she, too,
dozes off.*)

(*Patsy returns from the left.*)

PATSY: My inspection is complete. Nothing suspicious.
You can rest at ease! (*Coming close.*)
Asleep? Both of them? What's going on
here? (*He pours tea into the third cup and
sips it.*) Someone poured a sleeping draught
into this tea, a *mickey* as they say. Melvil
must be behind this. (*He sits at the table.*)
We'll soon see for sure! (*He pretends to doze
off.*)

(*Bobby enters quietly and carefully from the right.*)

BOBBY: (*after having looked around*) Here we go! The
drug's worked. (*He sees Patsy, but does not

100

recognize him.) Heavens, there's three of them! He must have served himself a cup of tea, too! But if there was enough for two, there was enough for three...

(*He goes to the table, looks at the three sleepers, raises George's arm which falls back down.*)

BOBBY: It's no sham! They're snoozing fast! Nothing beats that *mickey*! (*He takes a small a bottle of liquor from his jacket and takes a swig.*) As for me, I prefer this. (*He takes another swig.*)

PATSY: (*opening his eyes, aside, stupefied*) For goodness' sake! Is that Miss Deborah drinking from a bottle? Who can you trust?

(*Bobby takes a third swig.*)

PATSY: (*aside*) Again? That's not possible.

BOBBY: (*corking the bottle*) Enough. Got to be reasonable. When one has to work.

(*Patsy shuts his eyes.*)

BOBBY: I'm going to inform the Boss. (*He places the bottle on the table.*) Ah, they're having a fine sleep. (*He looks closely at Patsy.*) I know that mug! Where the Devil have I seen him? But my word, he's made up. (*He raises Patsy's hat and looks at his hair.*) He's got a wig.

(*Patsy suddenly gets up and gives Bobby a formidable blow sending him rolling on the ground.*)

PATSY: Hello, Bobby!

BOBBY: Patsy!

PATSY: (*with a new punch*) I said: hello, old buddy!

BOBBY: You, dirty rat!

(*Patsy continues beating up Bobby, who vainly tries to defend himself, but soon loses consciousness.*)

PATSY: Here, take this, pal! Ah, you like dressing up like a woman, now, eh? Gotcha! Had enough? Yes, I think so. (*He looks at George and Helen.*) They still haven't budged. Bobby surely isn't here all by himself. Melvil can't be far away!

(*Patsy drags the unconscious Bobby into the winter garden at the back. Meanwhile, Melvil quietly peeps out of the door at the left.*)

MELVIL: I thought I heard a fight. (*He notices Helen.*) Ah, there she is! She's sleeping. (*He goes close to her.*) How pretty she is! Ah, Helen! I will love you so much that you will eventually learn to love me.

(*Melvil takes her in his arms and prepares to carry her off. Suddenly, Carmen enters from the right, shaking*

with anger. Nick Carter enters after her and hides be-
hind the door.)

CARMEN: Liar!

MELVIL: (*stupefied*) Carmen!

CARMEN: Am I interrupting you?

MELVIL: (*hard*) What are you doing here?

CARMEN: You were counting on being alone with your
harlot? (*Pointing to Helen.*) But I was suspicious and here I am! You won't get rid of me
the way you got rid of Conegal, my lover,
whom you betrayed and gave up to the police
to have me for yourself. You loved me, then.

MELVIL: Shut up!

CARMEN: Now, you've had enough of me, but I haven't had enough of you. We're bound together, the two of us.

MELVIL: You're mad!

CARMEN: As long as I live, you'll never love anyone
else, you hear! (*She points her gun at Helen.*)

MELVIL: (*twisting her arm*) Drop that gun!

CARMEN: (*howling in pain*) Aaaah!

MELVIL: Drop it! (*Carmen lets her revolver fall.*) Foolish girl!

CARMEN: You love this girl.

MELVIL: Don't shout!

CARMEN: You already tried to kidnap her.

MELVIL: Someone will hear you.

CARMEN: Well, I swear it! If you deceive me, they'll learn how you betrayed Conegal. I have only one word to say to ruin you.

MELVIL: And, as for me, I have only one word to say to justify myself.

CARMEN: Say it. I defy you to say it.

MELVIL: (*pointing to Helen*) Yes, I already tried to kidnap her.

CARMEN: Ah, you admit it.

MELVIL: Because she's rich, very rich.

CARMEN: So are others.

MELVIL: Not like her. Today, I've got her, and not only her, who's worth 15 millions, but her aunt, who is worth 12 millions, her fiancé who is worth 20 millions, and even her old nurse, whom she'll ransom at a good price.

CARMEN: You're lying!

MELVIL: Look! (*He opens the crate.*) Those are already in the box. Do you believe me now? In one swoop, I'm kidnapping the entire household.

NICK: (*emerging from behind the curtain*) I gather this little explanation is over?

MELVIL: (*covering Nick with his revolver which he has drawn rapidly*) Nick Carter! May the Devil take you! (*He's about to shoot.*)

(*Patsy, who's been following the events from the garden, fires a shot that smashes Melvil's revolver in his hand. Melvil utters a scream of pain and drops the shattered gun.*)

MELVIL: Damn you!

PATSY: (*entering*) Hands in the air or I'll blow your brains out! (*To Carmen.*) And you, too, beautiful! Quick!

(*Melvil and Carmen raise their hands.*)

NICK: (*who has drawn his revolver*) Bravo, Patsy. You shoot like an angel.

(*Suddenly, Bobby emerges from the winter garden behind Patsy.*)

NICK: Watch out! Behind you! Who's that?

PATSY: That's Bobby Paddock!

NICK: (*to Bobby*) Halt! Hands in the air right away or I blow your head off!

(*Bobby raises his hands. Margaret and Deborah emerge from the crate, bewildered. Margaret notices Helen sleeping.*)

MARGARET: Ah, my God! Helen! (*She rushes to her niece.*)

DEBORAH: (*threatening Bobby with Carmen's gun, which she's picked up*) You scoundrel, give me back, my things!

(*She takes back her wig and her bonnet, which she places on her head, then her skirt and housecoat. Then, she goes to George and Helen. At that moment, Chick and Arizona Jack return.*)

CHICK: Melvil!

ARIZONA JACK: This is good!

NICK: (*to Melvil and Bobby*) You were brought in here in this box. You'll leave in this box! Come on, get in quick. I'll count to three and fire. One ! (*Bobby rushes in. Melvil with a slower step.*) Two!

MELVIL: I'll get even with you, Carter

NICK: Yes, yes. Meanwhile, lock the box, Patsy!

(*Patsy locks the crate.*)

CARMEN: (*wanting to rush to Melvil's help*) Forgive
me, my love!

CHICK: (*restraining her*) Don't budge, lady!

NICK: (*to Carmen*) For my part, I'm setting you free.
We're even. But don't cross my path again.

CARMEN: Nor you, mine. Goodbye!

(*Carmen leaves by the right.*)

NICK: (*to Chick and Arizona Jack*) Have you got a
hammer and nails?

CHICK: 'Twould be poor upholsterer that wouldn't.

(*Arizona Jack and Chick pull out hammers and nails.*)

ARIZONA JACK: (*singing*) Always keep a hammer in
your pocket

NICK: As for you, Chick, telephone the police to send a
van.

CHICK: Right away!

(*Chick leaves by the right.*)

NICK: As for you, Jack, nail up this box for me, solidly!

ARIZONA JACK: Whoop!

(*Nick goes to Helen.*)

MARGARET: (*to Nick*) They're still sleeping.

NICK: There's no danger! We'd better stretch them out. Where are their rooms?

DEBORAH: (*pointing to the back right*) This way!

NICK: (*to Arizona Jack*) You stay there, Jack, revolver in hand, without budging.

ARIZONA JACK: Count on me, Nick.

NICK: (*to Patsy*) Patsy, carry Miss Helen. As for me, I'll take the Lieutenant.

(*They carry them out, following Margaret and Deborah.*)

ARIZONA JACK: (*as he finishes nailing the box*) There! And if these two varmints escape, I'm ready! (*He pulls out an enormous revolver and sits on the ground, leaning against the box and starts singing:*)
> In the big old prairie
> The cowboy alone is king
> For him, it's his country
> Everything's ruled by him.
> The only thing on Earth he loves
> Are his rifle and his horse.

His life is lonely
But that's all the same to him
La, di, da–

(*As he sings, the rear of the crate slides quietly open. Unbeknownst to him, Melvil and Bobby emerge and leap out of the window. As Arizona Jack is beginning his* la, di, da, *Nick and Patsy reenter from the right and see the box empty. They rush to the cowboy and shake him roughly.*)

NICK: You idiot!

PATSY: Cretin!

NICK: Stupid ass!

ARIZONA JACK: (*speechless*) What? What? What's the matter?

NICK: (*pointing to the crate*) Look!

ARIZONA JACK: Damn it all! By all the imps of Devil's Mesa, I won't ever live this down! (*He tries to blow his brains out.*)

PATSY: Stop, imbecile! Enough being stupid!

ARIZONA JACK: (*furious*) I'm worse than a green-horn!

PATSY: Well, then– (*Pointing to the window.*) Run after them!

ARIZONA JACK: (*leaping out of the window*) Whoop!

NICK: Patsy, go to the police and ask for the file on Conegal.

PATSY: Carmen's former lover? Right!

NICK: Bring it to me.

PATSY: In an hour.

(*Patsy leaves by the right.*)

NICK: Damn! We've got to start all over again! Well! So be it!

CURTAIN

N.B. At theaters with police dogs at their disposal, the ending of this scene is as follows:

ARIZONA JACK: (*leaping out the window*) Whoop!

NICK: The dogs! Quick!

PATSY: Right away!

(*Patsy leaves by the back.*)

NICK (*aside*): Conegal–Carmen's former lover–I remember him now! Perhaps he has something to do with this. I'm going to reread his file.

(*Patsy returns with two dogs on a leash.*)

NICK: Let them smell the back of the crate and release them. I'll wait for you in the car.

(*Nick leaves by the right. Patsy does as ordered, then:*)

PATSY: Go, Max! Go, Duke!

(*The dogs leap out the window, followed by Patsy.*)

CURTAIN

The curtain must come up quickly on the next scene.

Scene IV. Melvil's Hideaway

The stage represents a deserted courtyard. At the back, there is a dark, old house. We see the ground floor, a door and two windows. The window on the left is open and usable. To the right, there is a wall, seven feet high. In the cutaway at the right, a door. To the left, another wall just like the one on the right, with a carriage door in the middle leading onto the street. In the left, in the cutaway, there is a shack and a wood pile enclosed by a plain gate.

The stage is empty. The roar of an automobile is heard. It stops on the left, in the street outside. Then there is the ringing of a bell. Mrs. Morris emerges from the house.

MRS. MORRIS: A car? Could it be...?

(*She goes to open the gate to the left. Melvil enters, followed by Bobby Paddock.*)

MELVIL: (*off, to the driver*) On your way! Go as fast as possible!

(*Melvil shuts the gate and the auto is heard leaving.*)

BOBBY: Hello, Mrs. Morris!

MRS. MORRIS: So it *is* you! I was scared. I thought it might be the police.

MELVIL: The police are on our heels.

BOBBY: Nick Carter and his dogs!

MRS. MORRIS: The Devil!

MELVIL: We've managed to escape them.

BOBBY: Not without trouble. We made many turns and detours.

MELVIL: Finally, we've lost them, that's the main thing. Lock the gate, Mrs. Morris.

MRS. MORRIS Yes, Boss.

(*She pushes the bolts in the gate.*)

BOBBY: (*to Melvil*) You think we're safe here?

MELVIL: No. We're not that far ahead of them. And if the dogs are still on our track, they'll follow the car.

BOBBY: Damn! So it's *bon voyage* then? Can we get a bit of refreshments before we go? I'm thirsty.

MRS. MORRIS: Come this way!

(*They go into the house.*)

BOBBY: Is Mr. Morris here?

MRS. MORRIS: Yes, he's inside.

MELVIL: (*aside*) To think that I had her, she was mine, I had her in my arms. Ah! That Carmen! She'll pay dearly for her treachery!

(*Melvil goes into the house. The stage is empty for several minutes. Suddenly, the two police dogs are seen crossing the wall at the left, and leaping into the courtyard. They go to the door of the house and, finding it closed, they leap through the open window. Soon, a disturbance can be heard inside the house. There are shouts from Bobby and the Morrises. The door opens and Melvil emerges. He goes to the shack and open its door, then hides behind it. The dogs come out of the house and rush into the shack. Melvil quickly shuts the door behind them. The dogs are trapped.*)

MELVIL: (*yelling*) Get going, Bobby!

BOBBY: I'm coming! I'm coming!

(*Bobby emerges from the house, holding his pants, the rear of it has been torn.*)

BOBBY: Ah, the nasty hounds! They bit me! They bit me!

(*Melvil and Bobby leave by the right cutaway. At the right, one hears the noise of an automobile, stopping. Nick jumps over the wall and lands in the courtyard.*)

Once there, he opens the door to the street. Patsy enters, followed by Arizona Jack. The hounds can be heard barking inside the shack. Nick opens the gate and releases them. Mrs. Morris then comes out of the house and fires a shot at the dogs, but she misses. The dogs rush at her and they would likely tear her apart if Patsy didn't call them off.)

NICK: (*to Mrs. Morris, now being held by Arizona Jack*) Melvil? Paddock? What's become of them? Where are they?

MRS. MORRIS: I've got nothing to say, copper!

PATSY: (*to the dogs*) Go, Max! Go, Duke, go!

(*The dogs leap over the wall at the right.*)

NICK: Quick! Get going!

(*They leave by the left. Their car can be heard leaving. The heretofore unseen Mr. Morris half-opens the door to the right and peeks outside.*)

MR. MORRIS: Are they gone?

CURTAIN

ACT III

Scene V. The Imperial Hotel

The stage is divided into two unequal sections: to the left, the lobby of the Imperial Hotel; to the right, a hotel room. The lobby: to the left, near the audience, the entrance, with the concierge's desk. To the back, a grand staircase and an elevator. Further back, a large door opening onto a salon. To the right, a door leading to the service area and, next to it, the check-in desk, with a telephone. There are potted plants and flowers all around. There is a partition separating the lobby portion of the stage (which is lit) from the hotel room's (which is not), with a door through it, that serves as the room's entry door. The room has a bed in the middle (one can easily get around it) and a dresser in the back. There are two chairs: one near the door and the other at the foot of the bed. Leaning against the partition is a console, surmounted by a mirror.

Melvil is dressed as a porter, wearing a red coat and a hat with the words "Imperial Hotel." He wears a fake blonde beard and speaks with a thick German accent. Mr. Van Burg, the Hotel Director, is a fat little man, quite animated, dressed in an elegant jacket, with a flower in its lapel. There are eight Maîtres' D dressed in uniform with white ties and napkins in hand, and a groom, also in uniform with a flat cap bearing the words "Imperial Hotel."

AT RISE, Melvil is seated behind the concierge's desk; the groom and the eight Maîtres' D are lined up in a row. Mr. Van Burg comes and goes in great agitation.

VAN BURG: (*to the Maîtres' D*) You're all swine, you hear me! Swine! Beat it! Get out of here! At once! You're fired!

(*They all leave.*)

MELVIL: (*very phlegmatic*) Come on, Mr. Van Burg, calm down. You're going to make yourself ill.

VAN BURG: (*swabbing his face with his handkerchief*) I'm choking with rage.

MELVIL: You've already got high blood pressure.

VAN BURG: It's abominable! Ah, the rascals!

MELVIL: (*still placid*) Yes, it's not nice.

VAN BURG: To go on strike in the midst of an evening party.

MELVIL: Indeed, it's not nice.

VAN BURG: And what a party! An engagement, a

splendid engagement, for which I'd booked this space! Eighty Reservations! All people of the highest society.

MELVIL: Luckily, the dinner is over.

VAN BURG: But the ball is going to start. A magnificent ball! And we have no one to pass the refreshments, to bus the tables, to bring up the carriages. Where can I find waiters at this hour?

MELVIL: (*still phlegmatic*) I could call my brother.

VAN BURG: Your brother?

MELVIL: Yes, he's an excellent Maître D. As soon as he's free, I could tell him to come here with his friends.

VAN BURG: Ah, Mr. Muller, my good Mr. Muller, you only got here yesterday and already, you save my life!

MELVIL: Oh, you are exaggerating, Mr. Van Burg!

VAN BURG: Quick! Call him!

MELVIL: At once. (*He goes to the telephone.*)

VAN BURG: I'm going to light up the rooms myself.

(*Van Burg leaves by the back.*)

MELVIL: (*pretending to call*) Hello! Hello!

(*After making certain Van Burg won't return, Melvil leaves the phone and goes quickly back to his desk. There, he takes a package and carries it to the hotel room, turning on the lights as he enters it. He puts the package in a drawer inside the dresser, then locks the drawer and places the key in his pocket. Meanwhile, Bobby Paddock, disguised as a coachman, enters the lobby from the left.*)

BOBBY: Heaven! Nobody's here! What can have happened to the boss?

(*Melvil emerges from the room, turning off the light behind him.*)

BOBBY: (*whistling softly*) Ah, there he is!

MELVIL: (*speaking in his natural voice*) Well Bobby? Has the ship arrived? Have you seen our man? Did you put him in a safe place?

BOBBY: Yes, the *Touraine* arrived, but Pelham wasn't amongst the passengers.

MELVIL: That's impossible!

BOBBY: I swear! I got out of my carriage to look at the faces of the passengers one by one, and I had the photograph that Carmen brought back from France. I can't have missed him. Pelham didn't disembark, I'm certain of it. And perhaps, it's better that way.

MELVIL: Why?

BOBBY: Because I wasn't the only one waiting for him.

MELVIL: Ah!

BOBBY: I recognized Miss Dodler's coachman hanging around and he, too, left grumbling. It might have gone badly for me if I'd tried to swindle him out of his client.

MELVIL: Give me back the photograph, I'll need it.

(*Bobby gives it to him.*)

BOBBY: By the way, did the strike go as planned?

MELVIL: It couldn't have been easier. The good Mr. Van Burg is eagerly awaiting you. Go get the others. And hurry up, we have no time to waste. I can't do a thing until your return.

BOBBY: I'll fly like a bird.

(*Bobby bows and leaves by the left.*)

MELVIL: If Pelham isn't coming, that's going to simplify things...

(*Van Burg enters from the back. We can see a well-lit, impressive dining-room through the door behind him.*)

VAN BURG: Well, Mr. Muller? Have you called your brother?

MELVIL: (*in a German accent*) *Ja*. He's coming with three or four of his friends. At this late hour, Mr. Van Burg, it's very lucky to have three friends within reach.

(*A messenger from the telegraph office enters by the left with a dispatch in his hand.*)

VAN BURG: Ah, some telegrams? Let's see. Thanks.

(*The messenger leaves.*)

VAN BURG: One, two, three–fifteen telegrams. All for the newlyweds. I'll deliver them in person.

MELVIL: For goodness' sake! You're the Director! I won't allow it. It's my job! Give them to me. (*aside*) I'll see if there's one from Pelham.

(*Melvil leaves by the right.*)

VAN BURG: Three Maîtres' D. What am I going to do with only three Maîtres' D for 80 persons. This will be hopeless!

(*Nick, Patsy, Chick and Arizona Jack enter by the left, disguised as policemen. Nick, wearing a sergeant's badge, is disguised to look fat, with a round, jovial and bright face. Patsy looks like an alcoholic. Chick is elegant. Arizona Jack, his hair and beard flaxen, sports a shrewd look.*)

NICK: (*in a thick, cordial voice*) Good evenin' t'ye!

VAN BURG: Policemen!

NICK: I'd like to see the manager.

VAN BURG: I'm the manager.

NICK: Mr. Van Burg?

VAN BURG: Myself. What do you want?

(*Nick signals his men, who post themselves at each door and remain on watch.*)

NICK: (*in his natural voice*) Listen to me, Mr. Van Burg. You're a discreet, resolute and courageous man, right?

VAN BURG: (*not reassured*) Why, certainly, certainly. Why do you ask me that?

NICK: I'm Nick Carter.

VAN BURG: Nick Carter? Ah, my God!

NICK: And these gentlemen are my assistants.

VAN BURG: (*uneasily*) What's going to happen?

NICK: We have need of you, Mr. Van Burg.

VAN BURG: Me? I've got to tell you–

NICK: Take it easy, you're not in any danger–

VAN BURG: (*relaxing*) Good, I like that, because–

NICK: (*smiling*) Yes, I see–

VAN BURG: Each to his own, right?

NICK: So you don't like danger?

VAN BURG: So long as it stays away from me as far as possible, I like danger fine.

NICK: I have serious reasons to believe that certain scoundrels of the worst sort are going to try to get in here tonight.

VAN BURG: (*his uneasiness returning*) Here?

NICK: For all I know, they may already be here.

VAN BURG: Thieves! They're after the wedding gifts!

NICK: I don't think so. The gifts are too well guarded.

VAN BURG: (*terrified*) Then, my silver! I've taken out my best silverware.

NICK: Well, keep your eyes open and if you see something suspicious, call me.

VAN BURG: Yes, Mr. Carter.

NICK: Don't use my name! No one must suspect my presence here. Call me "Sergeant." We'll need to search the place. The salons, the dining-rooms, the kitchens, the rooms. Don't be surprised and don't interfere. And, especially, keep your eyes open.

VAN BURG: Oh, I will!

NICK: Tradesmen, strangers, guests–everyone might be a suspect, understood? (*Van Burg recoils fearfully*.) What's wrong with you?

VAN BURG: Why, I'm being cautious. At the risk of being blunt, I don't know you. How do I know you're telling me the truth?

NICK: (*laughing*) Very good, Mr. Van Burg.

VAN BURG: You told me you're Nick Carter, but can you prove it?

NICK: Excellent! That's the way you ought to be, all right. (*He opens his tunic*.) Here's my badge. Are you satisfied? Now show me around! Where are the guests? The banquet must be over by now?

PATSY: (*at the rear*) I hear voices.

VAN BURG: They've just left the dining room. The ball is going to start.

NICK: Where is the room reserved for Mr. Pelham?

VAN BURG: Ah, you know?

NICK: Yes, I do.

VAN BURG: (*opening the door of the room adjacent*)
Here it is.

(*Van Burg turns on the light and goes in with Nick. The detective examines the room even looking under the bed. Van Burg looks impressed.*)

VAN BURG: (*aside*) He's like a dog on a scent.

NICK: (*pointing to a door*) What's over there?

VAN BURG: The bathroom.

(*Nick disappears.*)

VAN BURG: (*aside*) He's going to come out with bandits armed to the teeth.

(*Nick returns.*)

NICK: (*pointing to another door*) And over there?

VAN BURG: A small room.

(*Nick goes to inspect it.*)

VAN BURG: (*swabbing his face*) This is too much!

(*Nick returns and they go out, turning off the lights.*)

NICK: There's no other door than this one enabling access into this room?

VAN BURG: None.

NICK: Fine. Has everything so far gone well? Nothing unusual?

VAN BURG: No. (*excitedly*) Yes! Something incredible, unheard of, shocking, took place.

(*At a sign from Nick, Patsy and the others return.*)

NICK: What thing?

VAN BURG: After having served dinner, my Maîtres' D went on strike.

NICK: Bah!

VAN BURG: Without my dedicated concierge, I truly don't know what would have become of me.

NICK: What did he do?

VAN BURG: He telephoned his brother, who's a Maître D, and he's going to come with three of his friends.

NICK: Now, that's interesting. And where is this dedicated concierge?

VAN BURG: He went to deliver some telegrams.

NICK: Has he been in you employ a long while?

VAN BURG: No. Only since yesterday.

NICK: I see. What's his name?

VAN BURG: Muller. He's German. His predecessor fell ill rather suddenly and sent Muller to replace him. Now, if you'll excuse me, I must attend to refreshments.

NICK: Certainly, Mr. Van Burg.

VAN BURG: Until Muller's brother and his friends arrive, I'm going to be all by myself, and there are 80 guests to be served.

PATSY: (*to Nick*) What if we were to help him, Boss?

CHICK: Yes, good idea!

PATSY: That way, we could come and go everywhere without raising suspicion.

NICK: I suppose, in the case of a strike, one doesn't have a choice... (*To Van Burg.*) You'll explain the situation to your guests–if that suits you?

VAN BURG: I should say so, Mr. Carter. (*catching himself*) Sergeant! You're doing me a great service.

NICK: Well, then it's agreed.

ARIZONA JACK: Whoop!

NICK: (*severely*) Jack!

ARIZONA JACK: Pardon! It escaped me.

VAN BURG: Thanks again, thanks.

(*Van Burg leaves.*)

PATSY: What do you think of these Maîtres D's who scrammed at the last minute, Boss?

CHICK: And three others who were found to replace them in the nick of time?

ARIZONA JACK: By the brother of the concierge?

PATSY: It all looks pretty suspicious, huh?

ARIZONA JACK: I'll eat my hat if–

CHICK: Ah, no, enough!

PATSY: Eat it, and get it over with, once and for all.

NICK: All this's likely a set-up. But first, let's search the hotel. Patsy, take the elevator; Chick and Jack, the stairs. Inspect the corridors, the rooms, the offices, the kitchens, everything– minutely. As for me, I'll take a look at the salons and assure myself that the police and the insurance agents are guarding those precious gifts.

CHICK: Someone's coming.

NICK: Quick, beat it!

(*Patsy gets in the elevator; Chick and Arizona Jack leave by the stairs. The door at the back opens. The orchestra can be heard playing a waltz, and dancers can be seen swirling. Margaret Dodler enters from the back. She's now afflicted by a severe twitch in her right arm, to some comical effect.*)

MARGARET: Ah, I was looking for you!

NICK: And you've found me! Are you feeling safer now, Miss Dodler?

MARGARET: Not at all! The longer the party goes on, the more scared I become. Ah, what wouldn't I give for it to be over already?

NICK: Come on, show some courage! Have some faith!

MARGARET: I can't, it's stronger than I! Since the day those villains stuffed me inside that box, tied and gagged, I no longer live, I no longer sleep. I fear everything! I still hear that scoundrel's voice: "See that? It's my gun! If you make a racket, bang, I'll put a bullet in your coffee pot." My coffee pot! Ah, that voice. I'll never forget that voice as long as I live!

NICK: C'mon, Miss Dodler...

MARGARET: My dream now is to live guarded by two policemen, night and day.

NICK: Oh, surely you're exaggerating!

MARGARET: Don't leave me. Please, I beg you, don't leave me!

NICK: As little as possible, I promise you.

MARGARET: (*pointing to her right arm, twitching*) Living with this nervous twitch is a nightmare. I have to watch out when I eat. Yesterday, I nearly put out my eye with a fork!

NICK: Just your nerves, it will pass.

(*Helen Dodler, in her bridal gown, enters, followed by Van Burg.*)

HELEN: (*laughing*) Ah, it's amusing! Is it true, Mr. Carter?

NICK: Hush!

HELEN: Oh, pardon me! Is what Mr. Van Burg says true, Sergeant? Are your men going to serve us refreshments?

NICK: Yes, indeed–and we will try not to be too clumsy.

HELEN: I think you'll have a stunning success.

(*George Clancy enters at the back.*)

GEORGE: (*to Helen*) Why, you mustn't run off like this, Helen! Come back quickly, they're waiting for you!

HELEN: Coming, dear!

(*She leaves with George.*)

MARGARET: (*following Helen, to Nick*) I beg you not to leave me.

NICK: (*smiling*) I'm right behind you, I can't do more! You wouldn't expect me to give you my arm!

(*He leaves with Margaret, closing the door.*)

VAN BURG: Where's the concierge? Where's Muller?

(*Suddenly, he sees Melvil coming in from the right rear.*)

VAN BURG: Ah, there you are! You mustn't leave your station, Muller, especially this evening, you hear me? Not for any reason!

MELVIL: *Ja*!

VAN BURG: (*lowering his voice*) I have serious reasons to believe that scoundrels of the worst sort are going to attempt to get in here.

MELVIL: (*acting terrified*) Scoundrels, Mr. Van Burg?

VAN BURG: Of the worst sort. Perhaps they're here already!

MELVIL: *Mein Gott*!

VAN BURG: Are you brave, Muller?

MULLER: Oh, no, Mr. Van Burg, not at all!

VAN BURG: Ah, that's too bad!

MELVIL: I prefer to tell you the truth.

VAN BURG: (*with confidence*) As for me–I am!

MELVIL: I'm impressed!

VAN BURG: Keep your eyes open! And if you see anyone or anything suspicious, call me.

MELVIL: *Ja*! Now here's my brother.

(*Bobby enters from the left, followed by Jim, Sam and Carmen. The men are dressed as Maîtres D, white tie, black coats; Carmen is disguised as a groom with a blonde wig. All have disguised their faces. Bobby is slightly hunchbacked.*)

VAN BURG: At last! I was getting impatient!

BOBBY: (*in awkward, German-accented English*) We came with the greatest possible hurry.

VAN BURG: (*noticing Booby's hunch*) Oh, a hunch-back, eh? I don't like that very much.

BOBBY: Me either! I can't stand it, but strangely, there are women who like it. They say it brings good luck. My brother told me you were short of staff?

VAN BURG: Indeed.

MELVIL: (*to Bobby*) Such a good Boss he is, if you knew!

BOBBY: He seems to be. I also brought a groom. (*He points to Carmen.*)

VAN BURG: You did well. He will run the elevator and call for carriages.

CARMEN: Right, Boss!

VAN BURG: (*to Carmen*) Come with me, I'll get you a uniform and a cap. (*To Jim and Sam.*) You two gentlemen, you will take care of the platters and pass out the refreshments. (*To Melvil.*) And you, Muller, keep an eye for anyone suspicious–tradesmen, strangers, even guests.

MELVIL: Don't worry, Mr. Van Burg.

VAN BURG: (*to the others*) This way. Follow me.

(*Van Burg leaves by the back right, followed by Jim,*

Sam and Carmen.)

MELVIL: (*to Bobby*) You've reminded Jim and Sam of what we all agreed on?

BOBBY: Yes, don't worry. They know what to do. And I didn't tell Carmen a thing.

MELVIL: I'll give her my instructions myself. I've had since yesterday to study the hotel. We won't have any difficulties.

(*Carmen returns, wearing a uniform and a cap labeled "Imperial Hotel."*)

CARMEN: Van Burg's waiting for you, Bobby.

MELVIL: (*to Bobby*) Go and be sharp, very sharp. Carter's here with his men.

BOBBY: You've seen them?

MELVIL: No, but after the instructions that fool Van Burg just gave me, I'm sure he is.

BOBBY: We'll try to be meaner than they are.

(*Bobby leaves by the right rear.*)

CARMEN: Where are the wedding gifts?

MELVIL: They're in a small salon. There are heaps of pearls, precious stones, diamonds–more than a million dollars' worth.

CARMEN: Ah, if we can succeed!

MELVIL: That depends on you. A little audacity and it's a done deal.

CARMEN: Guarded?

MELVIL: By two policemen.

CARMEN: Ah!

MELVIL: But that's not your concern. At the signal, four of our men will jump on them and render them unconscious. As for me, I will keep everyone else occupied here. All you'll have to do is sweep up the jewels.

CARMEN: You can count on me!

MELVIL: To get yourself into the salon, you'll carry this telegram addressed to a Mr. Smithson that you'll be pretending to be trying to find. (*He gives her a telegram.*) Nothing simpler! Understood?

CARMEN: Yes, it's quite simple.

MELVIL: For the moment, stay here and don't move under any pretext.

CARMEN: Don't worry.

MELVIL: (*slowly lowering his voice*) Now, listen up. In ten minutes, you'll call Mr. Van Burg...

CARMEN: (*looking at her watch*) In ten minutes, yes.

MELVIL: You will tell him that Mr. Pelham has arrived and that he doesn't want anyone to know, except for the concierge who showed him to his room, and that he's in the process of changing his clothes before he goes to take part in the festivities.

CARMEN: Fine! At what time do I go to the salon for the jewels?

MELVIL: When I give you the signal.

CARMEN: You're quite certain there'll be no danger, despite the two policemen?

MELVIL: No, no danger at all! Go boldly, and correct your mistake of the other day.

CARMEN: (*tenderly*) Are you still thinking of that? You promised me to forget it!

MELVIL: I won't mention it again. Be smart and tonight we will all be rich. (*aside*) Tonight, my girl, you'll be sleeping in jail and I'll be rid of you!

(*Melvil goes into the room, turns the light on and takes out the package from the dresser. It contains a set of evening clothes and materials necessary for his transformation. He removes his costume, puts it in the drawer and then makes himself up as Pelham, consulting the photograph.*)

CARMEN: (*In the lobby*) Now I'm here in charge of the elevator! A million dollars! What luck! Where is that elevator? Upstairs! I've got to get it down. (*She presses the button and the elevator comes down.*)

(*Nick enters from the left, followed by Margaret.*)

NICK: (*without seeing Carmen, to Margaret*) Look, Miss Dodler, you must be reasonable.

CARMEN: (*aside*) Ah! That voice!

NICK: Stay in the ballroom. I've got to go from one place to another and I can't take you with me.

CARMEN: (*aside*) It's Nick Carter!

MARGARET: (*twitching*) I won't bother you, I promise you.

NICK: (*aside, noticing Carmen*) Heavens! A groom! (*Thickening his voice, to Carmen.*) Where do you come from? Are you in charge of the elevator?

CARMEN: (*lowering the pitch of her voice*) Yes, sir.

NICK: You weren't here before?

CARMEN: I've just returned from an errand.

NICK: I see! And the concierge, where is he? I've never seen him.

CARMEN: His nose was bleeding. I think he's in the courtyard.

NICK: His nose was bleeding?

CARMEN: Buckets. It took him suddenly.

NICK: (*aside*) Strange. (*To Margaret.*) Wait for me, I'll be back. (*aside*) I want to see that concierge.

(*Nick leaves by the back right.*)

CARMEN: (*aside*) Go on, my dear, search all you want! Try to find him!

MARGARET: Ah! My God, I'm trembling!

CARMEN: You are ill, Madame?

MARGARET: Yes, a little.

(*Bobby enters from the back, carrying refreshments and a napkin folded under the platter,*)

CARMEN: Here, have a drink. A glass of orange juice. That will fix you up.

MARGARET: Yes, you're right.

BOBBY: (*aside, recognizing Margaret*) Oh, it's her again!

(*He gives Margaret a glass of orange juice, but she has trouble grasping it because of her twitch.*)

MARGARET: No, I can't!

BOBBY: Allow me! (*He takes the glass and holds it to Margaret's lips so she can drink. Aside.*) I owe her that.

MARGARET: (*after having drunk*) Thanks!

BOBBY: That feels better, right? That way it went down?

MARGARET: (*recognizing Bobby's voice, staring at him, terrified*) Ah! It's him! It's him! The revolver! My coffee pot!

(*Margaret swoons into Carmen's arms.*)

BOBBY: Hot damn! She recognized me. We're done for. (*He puts down his platter and gags Margaret with his napkin.*) Quick! Open the elevator. (*Carmen opens the elevator and Bobby puts Margaret in and presses the button.*) Bye, bye! (*He waves goodbye.*) It's funny I cannot meet this lady without shoving her into a box.

CARMEN: Poor woman. (*She laughs.*)

BOBBY: (*laughing*) Yes, she's really got no luck. And there I was, thinking I was so well disguised!

How the Devil did she recognize me, damn it?

CARMEN: By your voice.

BOBBY: I didn't think of that.

CARMEN: You'd better be very careful. Nick Carter is not far.

BOBBY: You've seen him?

CARMEN: Just now. I was speaking to him. He's disguised as a policeman. A big, fat policeman.

BOBBY: Goodness! Say, that's not a dumb idea!

(*Patsy enters from the back right with a platter of refreshments.*)

CARMEN: Watch out! Another detective.

BOBBY: Again! It's raining cops!

PATSY: Who's that hunchback?

BOBBY: (*disguising his voice*) Now, monkey though I be, I am a man... But you, my poor friend, you look dull, so very dull!

PATSY: (*laughing, disguising his voice*) You think so?

BOBBY: Like a drunk taking the air. (*He points to Patsy's nose.*) Except for that beak of yours.

PATSY: Pretty, ain't it?

BOBBY: Superb! You must be able to sleep without a candle! They say you're a copper. You're into lemonade now? Things not going well at work?

PATSY: I've got to be doing a little of everything.

BOBBY: And the villains? What are you doing about them, in the meantime, the villains?

PATSY: This doesn't prevent me from keeping an eye on them.

BOBBY: You're a sly one, you are! Well, I like you. Let's have a toast!

PATSY: As you like.

(*He puts the platter down. Both take glasses.*)

BOBBY: Here's to a long life and a merry one! (*They drink.*) What's your name?

PATSY: Jerome. And you?

BOBBY: Luke. It seems to me I've seen you somewhere.

PATSY: Possibly. I don't recall seeing the back of you, tough.

BOBBY: Is it because of my hump you said that? I don't like being teased!

(*Bobby suddenly headbuts Patsy who falls behind the reception area into the adjacent office, off-stage. Bobby follows him. Meanwhile, Jim and Sam enter, holding platters and napkins.*)

CARMEN: (*to Jim and Sam*) Patsy's in there with a copper, quick! Go help him!

(*But Bobby emerges from the office, alone.*)

BOBBY: I think he had his score paid.

CARMEN: (*to Jim*) What did you just drop?

JIM: Drop?

CARMEN: Yes, from your napkin?

JIM: (*picking the object up*) Oh, nothing. (*Sly.*) A little gold purse that I just picked from a fat lady as she was drinking.

SAM: (*pulling things from his pockets*) As for me, I've got a brooch and some gold buttons.

CARMEN: If the Boss knew–

BOBBY: (*severely*) That's disgusting. The one time you're taken into society, you behave like a thief–

JIM: One's got to keep one's hands in practice.

BOBBY: (*smiling*) Me, I went for the watch and chain!
(*He pulls out a gold watch.*)

SAM: Damn Bobby!

(*They all laugh. Then, they pull themselves together and take their platters up.*)

BOBBY: Now, gentlemen, back to work. Let's spread through the salon. The ladies are thirsty.

(*They leave by the back left.*)

CARMEN: (*looking at her watch*) The ten minutes are up. Melvil must be ready. It's time to call Van Burg.

(*Suddenly, Nick and Van Burg enter back right.*)

NICK: (*to Carmen, thick voice*) You are playing with me, my little friend.

CARMEN: (*disguising her voice*) Me, sir?

NICK: The concierge isn't in the courtyard. Assuming he ever went there.

VAN BURG: (*to Carmen*) You didn't see him come back?

CARMEN: No, sir.

VAN BURG: It's incredible. After all the instructions I gave him.

(*Helen returns.*)

HELEN: (*to Nick*) Do you know where my aunt is? I can't find her.

NICK: I left her here just now.

CARMEN: The lady who was with you?

NICK: Yes, what became of her?

CARMEN: She drank a glass of orange juice and went back to the ballroom through here. (*She points to the door at the left back.*)

(*Harry Pelham enters from the left door closer to the audience. He wears glasses and carries a valise in his hand. Nick and Helen look at him.*)

VAN BURG: Who might you be, sir?

CARMEN: (*aside, terrified*) My God! It's Pelham!

PELHAM: My name is Harry Pelham. You should have a room reserved for me.

HELEN: (*rushing to him*) Godfather! Ah, how happy I am to see you!

PELHAM: Helen!

HELEN: Yes, it's me! (*They kiss and hug.*)

CARMEN: (*aside*) I've got to warn Melvil!

PELHAM: My dear little Helen. How pretty you are!

CARMEN: I'll take your suitcase, sir. (*She takes it from him.*)

VAN BURG: Take it into that room.

CARMEN: Yes, sir.

(*She goes into the room at the right.*)

PELHAM: Let me look at you and kiss you. (*More kissing.*)

NICK: (*to Van Burg*) So, what happened to Muller, your concierge? Where is he?

(*Nick leaves with Van Burg to the left. Meanwhile, inside the room, Melvil was just about ready when Carmen enters and whispers to him.*)

MELVIL: (*lowering his voice*) The Devil! It's not possible.

CARMEN: (*low*) He just arrived; he's there–in the lobby. Here's his suitcase. (*She puts it on the floor.*)

MELVIL: (*harshly*) That's fine! Get out of here!

CARMEN: What are you going to do?

MELVIL: Leave me alone!

CARMEN: Should I still–

MELVIL: (*furiously*) Nothing has changed! Nothing! Get out of here!

(*Carmen leaves the room and takes back her place next to the elevator. Melvil thrusts everything into the dresser, takes his gun and dagger and hides inside the bathroom at the right.*)

PELHAM: (*to Helen*) So you're married ! Happy?

HELEN: Yes, very. I can't wait to introduce you to my husband.

PELHAM: In a minute. First, let me change clothes.

(*Van Burg enters left, near the audience. He opens the door to the room for Pelham and ushers him inside. Helen follows them.*)

CARMEN: (*aside*) They're going to see Melvil!

VAN BURG: (*showing the room*) Over here, the bathroom, with hot and cold water.

PELHAM: (*pointing to the door near the bed*) And what's over there?

VAN BURG: A small office.

PELHAM: Very nice.

VAN BURG: Do you need anything else?

PELHAM: No, thank you. If I do, I'll ring.

(*Van Burg leaves the room and closes the door behind him.*)

VAN BURG: (*to Carmen*) Mr. Muller hasn't returned yet?

CARMEN: No, I haven't seen him.

VAN BURG: It's incredible. Where can he be?

(*Van Burg leaves by the back right.*)

CARMEN: (*aside*) What's going to happen in there?

PELHAM: (*to Helen*) It's been such a long time! You were only a child when I left you. I can still see you in a short dress, and your hair in tresses. And be honest, you don't remember me too well, eh?

HELEN: I'm sorry, Godfather!

PELHAM: (*laughing*) That's all right!

HELEN: I remember three things about you: your big beard, your glasses and the big diamond ring I still see on your finger. But I also never forgot your kindness, which I often abused, along with your cheeriness and tenderness.

PELHAM: My dear girl!

HELEN: I often felt very keenly that you loved me like your own daughter.

PELHAM: Yes, like the daughter I never had!

HELEN: So I was really sad this morning when I saw you weren't here for my wedding.

PELHAM: (*opening his suitcase from which he removes his clothes*) It wasn't my fault, my pretty. A disabled engine immobilized us for 48 hours.

HELEN: How come you didn't disembark with the other passengers?

PELHAM: That was because of your friend Nick Carter. Yesterday, he sent me a wireless instructing me not to leave the ship until a half-hour after everybody else. I didn't understand why, but I complied.

HELEN: Then, I forgive you.

PELHAM: Thank you. You know, I've brought you my own wedding gift.

HELEN: Ah!

PELHAM: It's here in my suitcase.

HELEN: What is it? Can I see it?

PELHAM: A bit of patience, curious girl. I'll give it to you soon. Let me get dressed first.

HELEN: Hurry!

PELHAM: In five minutes, I'll be ready.

HELEN: (*embracing him*) This is for the nicest gift that I haven't yet seen.

PELHAM: So you think it's nice?

HELEN: I am certain of it, my beloved godfather.

(*Helen leaves the room. Carmen only has time to make herself scarce. Helen leaves by the back left. Then Carmen returns to the elevator.*

(*Inside the room, Pelham takes off his coat. Taking a comb, he combs his beard, looking at himself in the mirror over the dresser. Suddenly, Melvil comes out of the bathroom, dagger in hand, and tiptoes behind Pelham, but the latter sees him in the mirror and turns around. Melvil hides his weapon behind his back. The two men look at each other.*

(*Meanwhile, in the lobby, the big door at the back opens. Eight groomsmen and bridesmaids, beflowered and be-ribboned in white, enter dancing a four step, and circle around the stage several times. Other guests remain in the hall at the back, applauding, laughing, observing.*

(*Inside the room, Melvil rushes on Pelham, plunges his dagger into his heart and kills him swiftly. He leaves the weapon in the wound. Then he sits the body in an armchair facing the public, bolts the door and takes out his makeup kit. He sits in a chair, facing the cadaver, a small mirror in his hand, and continues to apply his own makeup. Then, he takes the glasses from Pelham's body and puts them on. After that, he takes the dead man's ring, etc. Once finished, Melvil drags Pelham's body into the bathroom and locks the door. He then goes to the suitcase on the bed, finds a jewel box inside, which he opens and places in his pocket.*)

(*The dancers leave by the back. Helen returns.*)

HELEN: Where is Aunt Margaret? What's become of her? (*To Carmen.*) Has the lady who drank a glass of orange juice returned?

CARMEN: No, Miss.

(*Melvil, disguised as Pelham, emerges from the room.*)

HELEN: (*going to him*) I'm very concerned.

MELVIL: (*imitating Pelham's voice*) What's the matter, child?

HELEN: Aunt Margaret has disappeared! Something has certainly happened to her.

(*Melvil signals to Carmen; she leaves by the left back, her fake telegram in hand.*)

150

MELVIL: What do you mean, something has happened to her?

HELEN: She's been a bit ill for some time. I'm afraid she's badly off.

MELVIL: She's probably resting in some quiet corner. Or perhaps, she went out to get some air. The evening is so superb!

(*Nick enters left front.*)

HELEN: You think so?

MELVIL: No question. Rest easy!

NICK: Impossible to put my hand on that damned concierge. (*To Helen.*) I beg you to introduce me to Mr. Pelham.

HELEN: Gladly. Godfather, this is police sergeant–

NICK: No really. Come on!

HELEN: You warned me not to utter your name!

NICK: You can't be serious!

HELEN: As you wish, then. (*To Melvil/Pelham.*) This is our great friend, Mr. Nick Carter! My godfather, Mr. Harry Pelham!

MELVIL: (*shaking Nick's hand*) Who thanks you for the warning that you sent him.

NICK: It pays to be cautious.

MELVIL: I'm delighted to make your acquaintance, Mr. Carter! You are famous everywhere, even in France, where I'm coming from, and where all the newspapers have brought me tales of your incredible exploits.

NICK: You are much too kind, Mr. Pelham. (*aside*) Oh, his eyes!

MELVIL: It seems that no villain escapes you and that, most of the time, the police is powerless.

NICK: Well, let's not exaggerate! (*aside*) He's got the same eyes as Melvil.

MELVIL: It must be quite a thrill, eh? Being a man-hunter?

NICK: Sometimes. It depends on the game! (*aside*) I must be going mad! I'm seeing Fantômas everywhere now.

MELVIL: It seems to me I would love those emotions.

NICK: As a hunter or as game?

MELVIL: As a hunter, of course! Although, to tell the truth, the game ought to be enjoying himself also, especially when he's laughing at the hunter?

NICK: Oh, he won't be laughing for long.

MELVIL: Hum! That depends on the game, as you were saying just now. And on the hunter, too, naturally.

NICK: (*aside*) My word; one would say he's laughing at me!

MELVIL: (*to Helen*) Here, my dear heart, here's my wedding gift.

(*He takes the jewel box out and gives it to her.*)

HELEN: (*opening it*) A pearl necklace! I've never seen one this beautiful.

NICK: It's royal!

MELVIL: I am still your beloved godfather?

HELEN: How you spoil me.

MELVIL: I love you so much.

HELEN: Me, too, I really love you. (*She kisses him.*)

NICK: (*aside*) No, truly, I must be a fool.

(*Van Burg enters from the right at the rear.*)

NICK: Ah, Mr. Van Burg–

MELVIL: (*embracing Helen*) My dear little girl– (*Sud-

denly, Helen recoils instinctively.) What's the matter with you?

HELEN: I–I don't know exactly. I don't know how to say it–you no longer seem the same to me.

MELVIL: What are you saying? I'm your kindly godfather Harry with his big beard, his glasses and his big diamond ring on his finger...

NICK: This is unacceptable, Mr. Van Burg. A concierge doesn't vanish into thin air like this without a reason.

VAN BURG: I don't understand at all.

NICK: (*looking at the elevator*) Who was using the elevator?

VAN BURG: I don't know.

NICK: Call it down.

VAN BURG: Right away. (*He presses the button.*)

NICK: (*looking all around*) Where could he be hiding?

(*Suddenly, he notices the door leading towards the office, which is closed. He goes there, opens it and goes inside. Meanwhile, Bobby returns back left. Melvil signals him and Bobby exits back right.*)

MELVIL: (*leading Helen to the left*) Come with me. I'll tell you stories about my life in Normandy...

NICK: (*from the office*) Ah! Patsy!

VAN BURG: (*looking inside the elevator*) Heavens!
Miss Dodler!

(*Suddenly, all the lights go off. We hear various exclamations from the guests. Melvil seizes Helen and, with
one hand over her mouth, drags her to the left.*)

HELEN: (*screaming faintly in the corridor*) Help! Help!

VAN BURG: What is this? A short circuit?

(*Nick emerges from the office with a flashlight.*)

NICK: They shorted the fuse box. Where is it?

VAN BURG: I know where it is. I'll fix it!

(*He leaves running by the rear right.*)

NICK: I've been tricked! Fool that I am!

(*The door to the salon opens and the guests can be seen
lighting up matches. George Clancy comes in from the
back.*)

GEORGE: What's going on?

NICK: (*lying*) Nothing! A short circuit.

(*The lights come back. There are shouts of satisfaction
by the guests. Nick locks the back door.*)

GEORGE: (*noticing Margaret in the elevator*) Ah, Miss Margaret! There you are! Helen was looking for you...

(*He goes to her as does Van Burg, who's just returned. They take her to sit down; she's fainted. Carmen enters from the left, held by two policemen, followed by Chick and Arizona Jack. Her head is uncovered; her dark hair is loose and floating on her back; her uniform was torn in the struggle.*)

CHICK: (*pushing Carmen*) Come on, move!

NICK: (*recognizing her*) Carmen!

ARIZONA JACK: We caught her trying to steal the wedding gifts.

NICK: Handcuff her.

(*The policemen put cuffs on Carmen.*)

GEORGE: (*to Van Burg*) I must tell Helen.

(*George leaves hurriedly by the back.*)

CARMEN: (*furious*) Ah, the coward! The dirty rat! He threw me into the hands of the police.

(*Patsy emerges from the office, staggering. Chick goes to him*)

CHICK: Patsy! Are you hurt?

PATSY: No, just a bit dazed. It's nothing. (*He sits down.*)

CARMEN: (*furious, weeping with rage*) You were right, Nick Carter! He no longer loves me! He was the one who betrayed me. As he did with Conegal! He's abandoned me! He's mad for that girl! But I will avenge myself! Ah, yes, I will avenge myself!

(*George returns hurriedly, several guests in tow. They go to Margaret's side.*)

GEORGE: Helen! Where is Helen? She's gone!

CARMEN: Melvil has her!

GEORGE: Melvil!

CARMEN: (*still mad with rage*) He adores her–or her money! I don't know which he loves most!

VAN BURG: But that's impossible. Mrs. Clancy was here, just now, with her godfather, Mr. Pelham.

CARMEN: No–with Melvil–Muller–your concierge, you fool!

NICK: I'll be–! I suspected as much!

(*He goes back to the room, breaks the lock on the bathroom door and goes inside.*)

GEORGE: My wife! In the hands of that bandit!

(*Nick returns, very pale.*)

NICK: There, in the bathroom–Mr. Pelham–murdered–a dagger through his heart.

VAN BURG: Great God!

GEORGE: (*semi-hysterical*) Where are they? I demand to know where they are!

CARMEN: At Meltcraft's tavern in Chatham Square, the Rat Trap.

NICK: (*to the police*) Take her away!

CARMEN: Kill him! Kill the coward! Kill Melvil!

(*She leaves screaming, dragged by the police, by the left front.*)

GEORGE: My wife! My dear wife!

NICK: Courage! All hope is not lost!

GEORGE: Ah, please, save her, Mr. Carter! Save her!

NICK: For sure, we'll save her–or die trying. Come!

(*They leave as Margaret finally comes to.*)

CURTAIN

ACT IV

Scene VI. The Rat Trap

The stage represents a huge cellar whose furnishings resemble the dining room of a ship. The walls are completely paneled in wood are covered in such a way that the doors cannot be seen. The panels are themselves adorned with large iron buttons and, by pushing some of them, hidden doors can be opened. There's a door to the right, leading to other rooms in the tavern; a door to the back right, which opens on a secret corridor, a door to the back center, opening onto another room, and finally, a door to the left, midway to the audience. Near the audience, also on the left, there is a high counter surrounded by a large leather bar filled with bottles. The length of the wall behind the counter contains shelves filled with bottles. Also to the left, in cutaway, there is a small, low platform reached by a single step. Beneath that platform are five large, leather collars screwed into the wall, with hanging chains. Further back, there is a piano. The tables are surrounded by chairs and benches on each side of a central aisle. There are portraits of famous gangsters hanging from the walls. About half of the lights are not lit.

*AT RISE, Meltcraft is arranging glasses and bottles be-
hind and under the counter. He has a bestial head and is
in shirtsleeves, with his sleeves rolled up. Catherine enters from the right, near the audience, still pretentiously
dressed and made up. She carries an armful of pretty
flowers.*

CATHERINE: Are you here, Mr. Meltcraft?

MELTCRAFT: (*who was down beneath the counter*)
Who's calling me?

CATHERINE: (*simpering*) Ah, good evening, Mr. Meltcraft!

MELTCRAFT: Hey, it's Miss Catherine, the beauty of
beauties. Good evening, honey-pot.

CATHERINE: Always gallant, Mr. Meltcraft.

MELTCRAFT: At your service, my jewel! What will
you have? Gin? Rum? It's on the house!

CATHERINE: You're too kind, Mr. Meltcraft! A dab of
gin then.

MELTCRAFT: At your command, princess. (*He pours
two small glasses.*)

CATHERINE: (*looking at the room*) What a funny-
looking room!

MELTCRAFT: You've never been down here before?

CATHERINE: No, I've always seen you upstairs.

MELTCRAFT: This cellar is for our regulars only. They turn up here from midnight to 5 a.m. and they don't get bored, I beg you to believe! They drink, they sing, they dance! It's rather joyous!

CATHERINE: (*pointing to the portrait*) Ah, that mug. Who's he? He frightens me.

MELTCRAFT: A strapping fellow. The Slasher. Tom Perkins. The old Boss, the one Mr. Melvil replaced.

CATHERINE: The Slasher! Brrr!

MELTCRAFT: He's been in the slammer for the last 13 years and he'll remain there for the rest of his life.

CATHERINE: I won't be the one visiting him there. He's too ugly. (*drinking*) To your health, Mr. Meltcraft.

MELTCRAFT: To our love, my treasure!

CATHERINE: Will you kindly shut up, you bad man, you! You'll get me to start believing you. (*They drink and clink glasses.*) Have you prepared everything for the Boss?

MELTCRAFT: The room is ready, yes. The one in the back, the largest one.

CATHERINE: The small suitcase I sent you?

MELTCRAFT: I placed it by the chimney. What time's Mr. Melvil gonna be here?

CATHERINE: I don't know exactly. He told me to expect him around 10.

MELTCRAFT: Those flowers are for him?

CATHERINE: They're for his honey. He's just kidnapped her. She got married this morning.

MELTCRAFT: And kidnapped the same evening! Sonofagun! Now there's an exciting day!

CATHERINE: Ah, she won't be lacking in excitement, for sure. I'm going to prepare everything for the lovebirds. (*She goes to the back.*) Where's the door to the room? I don't see any door!

MELTCRAFT: (*laughing*) There are no doors in my cellar, or at least, they're invisible. To open them, you've got to push certain buttons that only my customers know. (*He pushes a button and a door opens.*) There, you see? You can get in this cellar, but you can't easily get out. That way, if a cop, or a spy, or a traitor, slips in here, he can't escape his punishment by fleeing.

CATHERINE: What punishment?

(*Meltcraft pushes another button and a door on the left opens.*)

MELTCRAFT: If we catch him here, we throw him into the Rat Trap. There!

CATHERINE: (*looking out*) Oh, how dark it is!

MELTCRAFT: There's a stairway with five steps at the bottom of which runs a large sewer. The fifth step moves. Any man who sets foot on it is lost.

CATHERINE: Ah, what a death! It's horrible!

MELTCRAFT: If you want to see it for yourself (*He pushes her, laughing.*)

CATHERINE: (*recoiling*) Ah! No, thanks!

MELTCRAFT: If there are several of them, you tie 'em to the rings you see attached to the wall. Then, you uncork this gas pipe, and it's good night sweetheart!

CATHERINE: (*terrified*) My God!

(*Francis enters from the right near the audience, carrying two crates of bottles.*)

MELTCRAFT: (*to Francis*) Will you hurry up, you Goddamn dawdler!

FRANCIS: Greetings, Miss Catherine.

MELTCRAFT: Where have you been? You know very well I've been waiting for you so I can go to bed!

CATHERINE: You're going to bed already?

MELTCRAFT: Yes, indeed! Every evening, from 10 to midnight. Without a nap, I couldn't keep going. Goodnight, my darling. I'll dream of you.

CATHERINE: (*simpering*) Oh, Mr. Meltcraft!

MELTCRAFT: (*aside*) More likely, having nightmares.

(*Meltcraft leaves by the right near the audience. Catherine enters the room at the back. Francis arranges the bottles behind the bar. Then, Catherine returns, without the flowers.*)

CATHERINE: Mr. Francis?

FRANCIS: Yes, Miss Catherine?

CATHERINE: Would you be kind enough to let me know when the Boss gets here?

(*Bobby Paddock furtively opens the door at the back right.*)

BOBBY: Psst!

CATHERINE: Ah, Mr. Paddock!

BOBBY: Can I come in?

CATHERINE: Yes, everything's ready.

(*Bobby disappears.*)

CATHERINE: Get out, Mr. Francis. The Boss doesn't
want anybody here. He actually ordered me–

FRANCIS: Right. I'm off!

(*Francis leaves by the right near the audience.*)

CATHERINE: Ah, here they are!

(*Melvil enters by the right rear, carrying Helen who is
unconscious. Bobby, Jim and Sam follow him. Catherine
brings up a chair in which Melvil places Helen.*)

BOBBY: Still unconscious?

MELVIL: Yes.

CATHERINE: How pretty she is.

MELVIL: Do you have a bottle of salts?

CATHERINE: Yes.

MELVIL: Get her to breathe them. (*To Bobby, Jim and
Sam.*) Get back to the hotel and make very
sure you're not recognized.

BOBBY: Don't worry!

MELVIL: Bobby, find out what happened to Carmen.

BOBBY: OK!

MELVIL: What she told Carter. What they did. Got it?

BOBBY: Yes, Boss.

SAM: For sure.

JIM: Easy.

MELVIL: Go!

(*Bobby, Jim and Sam leave the way they came.*)

CATHERINE: She just sighed.

(*Melvil kisses Helen's hand lovingly.*)

MELVIL: (*to Catherine*) My clothes are in the room?

CATHERINE: Yes, in the suitcase.

MELVIL: Watch over her; don't move. I'll be back.

(*He goes into the room at back.*)

CATHERINE: She's opening her eyes. What beautiful peepers! (*To Helen.*) Well, feeling any better, my pretty?

HELEN: (*looking around her*) Where am I?

CATHERINE: At Mr. Meltcraft's, my lovely. A worthy man. The owner of this beautiful saloon. You want something to drink?

HELEN: No thank you.

CATHERINE: (*going to the counter*) Well, I do. You should have some, too. A little drink never harmed anyone. (*She pours two glasses of gin.*) The two of us are going to click.

HELEN: (*aside*) Great God! I remember! I remember! George! George!

(*Helen bursts out weeping, her head in her hands.*)

CATHERINE: (*returning with two glasses*) The gin here is perhaps a bit strong, but there's nothing better to help you get back on your feet. (*She offers Helen a glass.*) Here's to you! What? You're crying! Look here, you mustn't cry. There's nothing to cry about. (*She drinks her drink and puts both on the table.*)

HELEN: (*in tears, rising*) I want to leave! I want to leave!

(*Helen looks around for a way out.*)

CATHERINE: Well, you can't, my lovely. That's all there is to it!

HELEN: (*wildly*) Where is the door?

CATHERINE: There isn't any.

HELEN: I beg you, help me! Have pity on me!

CATHERINE: Look, my pretty, calm down! You're going to make yourself ill.

HELEN: Let me leave! I want to leave! I'll give you all the money you want. You'll be rich!

CATHERINE: I'd gladly do it, but I can't.

HELEN: (*sitting down and starting to cry again*) This is horrible! Horrible! Ah, I want to die!

CATHERINE: For goodness' sake, will you shut up! Don't be stupid! You're young and pretty. Don't make yourself ill. You've got nothing to fear. You're the one with the upper hand here. The Boss loves you. You can get him to do anything you want. Ah, I know more than one gal who would love to be in your shoes! He's so handsome, so distinguished–come on, don't cry! I don't want you to cry! What good does it do you?

HELEN: (*calming down and making a decision*) You're right: it's no use at all!

CATHERINE: It makes your eyes red, that's all! And that would be a shame.

HELEN: The very day of my marriage, of my happi-
ness–to be torn from all that's dear to me...

CATHERINE: Well, yes–when you're not expecting it.

HELEN: To be in the power of this wretch.

CATHERINE: Mr. Melvil? Oh, for the love of God!

(*Melvil enters dressed as in the first act.*)

MELVIL: Leave us, Catherine.

(*At the sound of Melvil's voice, Catherine rises excitedly.*)

CATHERINE: You've got no more need of me, Boss?

MELVIL: No, you may go! Tomorrow morning at 8
a.m., come to the Red House.

CATHERINE: I will.

(*Catherine leaves by the right, near the audience.*)

MELVIL: Will you ever forgive me, Miss Dodler?

HELEN: (*haughtily*) I now am Mrs. George Clancy.

MELVIL: Will you pardon me for the somewhat brutal
manner in which–

HELEN: The manner of a wretch and a coward.

MELVIL: The manner of a man who adores you, who was going to lose you, and who had no other means of conquering you–

HELEN: (*scornfully*) Anyway, I know you now. I know who you are and nothing about you would surprise me.

MELVIL: Here's what I must tell you! Yes, you are mine, and yes, I will keep you against all, but you have nothing to fear. No force, no violence. I give you my word! I love you deeply, with a burning, respectful love. After you love me, you, too, will–

HELEN: (*revolted*) Me? Love you?

MELVIL: (*even more passionate*) Yes, you will love me, I am sure of it. My love is too strong, too sincere–

HELEN: I scorn you and I hate you!

MELVIL: You will love me, Helen! You will forget my brutality. My fervor and my love will absolve me. But I won't take you, except of your own free will. The feeling that you inspired in me from the day I first saw you– This feeling, so new to me, so foreign to my nature, is too precious and too dear for me to want to destroy it. You are, and to my eyes you will remain, infinitely beautiful and pure. You will be my sole joy, my only reason to live, and I will surround you with so much care, devotion and love that your heart will eventually soften and you will turn towards me and reciprocate my feelings! What does it matter what I have been until now? What does my life matter? What matter my crimes? A single thing exists, one alone: I love you and you will love me.

HELEN: Never!

MELVIL: (*opening the door at the back*) Here's your room. Go to it without fear, and rest in all security. This place is not very respectable, but it is safe! We'll leave tomorrow! Tonight, I'm afraid the company will be a bit noisy, a bit rowdy. Although you will be able to hear them, don't be afraid, because the bolt on your door is solid. As for me, I'll be here, and if you want something–

HELEN: Yes, I do.

MELVIL: What? Speak.

HELEN: A weapon.

MELVIL: A weapon? Against me?

HELEN: I want to be able to defend myself.

MELVIL: You don't trust my word?

HELEN: No.

171

MELVIL: Take my revolver then! (*He gives it to her.*) If you detest me to that degree, kill me now. You can do it.

HELEN: No, I will not dirty myself by killing you. Someone else will take care of you!

MELVIL: Someone else? Who?

HELEN: The executioner!

(*She goes to her room and bolts the door behind her. Overwhelmed, Melvil falls into a chair.*)

CURTAIN

The curtain must come up quickly on the next scene.

Scene VII. The Rat Trap (cont'd)

Same set. All the lights are on. The room is filled with customers of all types, dressed in the most disparate manner, elegant and casual. Chinese, Japanese, Italian, Mexican, Irish, Middle-Easterners, etc. There are also girls in frilly costumes. Everyone is drinking, smoking, gambling, shouting and arguing. Four waiters come and go serving the customers.

AT RISE, Melvil is seated at a table near the door at the back. Patsy Murphy and George Clancy, disguised as sailors, are playing cards at a table on the left, near the door. Chick Carter and Arizona Jack, disguised as lowlives, roll dices at a table to the right. The roar of the conversations is deafening. On the platform, a woman dances to the accompaniment of a piano and public applause.

OSWALD: (*a customer seated to the right, applauding*)
          Bravo, Tomato! Bravo, my girl!

WILLIAMS: (*seated next to Oswald*) She is stunning!

PEDRO: (*an elegant man seated to the left, shouting*)
          More champagne, Francis!

FRANCIS: Coming, coming!

WILLIAMS: What legs!

OSWALD: And that butt! Take a gander at that!

(*The dance stops. Thunderous applause and bravoes. The girl bows and comes off the platform. The pianist continues to play, and at various intervals, dinners are being served.*)

WILLIAMS: C'mere, Tomato! Come, my good Tomato!

OSWALD: A number like that must warm you up–

WILLIAM: What will you have? Champagne?

(*Tomato sits at the table with them.*)

OSWALD: (*shouting*) Francis! Champagne!

FRANCIS: Coming, coming!

GEORGE: (*low to Patsy*) You really think she's here?

PATSY: For me, there's not a shadow of a doubt. Melvil's back there. No, don't turn you, he's watching us.

GEORGE: Poor Helen!

PATSY: Come on! Courage, Lieutenant. The hardest part's done. We've managed to infiltrate this dive, and Nick Carter will prevail–as he always does! He's going to be here soon! Let's wait for him.

(*They continue to play. Bobby, Jim and Sam enter. Melvil goes to them.*)

MELVIL: (*low*) So? What have you found?

BOBBY: Carmen got nabbed!

MELVIL: (*satisfied*) Ah! How did it happen?

BOBBY: She tried to snatch the wedding gifts and fell into the hands of the coppers who took her away.

MELVIL: And Carter? What did they say? What did they do after our departure?

JIM: As to that, no one could give us any information.

BOBBY: In any case, tonight we can relax.

MELVIL: And tomorrow, we'll be safe. Come this way.

(*Melvil leads them to a table at the back.*)

ARIZONA JACK: (*low to Chick*) Did you spot them?

CHICK: (*low*) The whole gang is here!

ARIZONA JACK: Things are going to get hot and heavy here very soon.

(*They continue to play. Meanwhile, Tomato has gone to sit next to Pedro, who tries kissing her.*)

TOMATO: (*pushing him away*) Ah, leave me alone!

PEDRO: But I adore you, my little Tomato!

TOMATO: Well, *you* bore *me*.

PEDRO: What? No more love? (*shouting*) Francis! More champagne!

FRANCIS: Coming, coming!

(*Tippett, an elegant young man, completely drunk, gets up on the platform and starts singing in a lachrymose and off-key voice.*)

TIPPETT: I didn't know what love was...

(*Hoots and protests.*)

TIPPETT: ...Until I met VAL-EN-TINE!

VARIOUS VOICES: Ah, no! Enough! Shut him up! Plug it! Kick him out!

TIPPETT: (*starting over with the stubbornness of the intoxicated*) I didn't know what love was...

VOICES: Lucky for her! Zip it! Go to bed! Make him stop! Shut it or I smash it!

TIPPETT: (*maudlin*) Bunch of showoffs! (*He starts*

singing again.) I didn't know–

(*Several men jump on stage, grab him and force him to sit down despite his protests. A quarrel breaks out between Otto and Jacoby who have been playing cards. Otto grabs Jacoby by the throat.*)

OTTO: (*drunk*) You dirty swine!

JACOBY: Lemme go!

OTTO: You were cheating me!

JACOBY: Lemme go or I'm gonna hit you.

OTTO: Give me back my money!

(*Meltcraft enters.*)

MELTCRAFT: (*intervening*) Enough, you two! No fighting in here, get it? You know the rules! What's wrong?

OTTO: He stole 20 dollars from me.

JACOBY: That's not true.

MELTCRAFT: (*to Jacoby*) Give him back ten.

JACOBY: Why should I? I won fair and square!

MELTCRAFT: Give him back ten dollars right now or I'll have you kicked out of here and you'll never set foot in here again. Your choice!

JACOBY: (*tossing money on the table*) Here, you dirty drunk! There's your money! But it's unfair all the same, since I won it honestly.

OTTO: It was 20 he did me out of.

MELTCRAFT: And you only get ten back. That'll teach you a lesson: when you're drunk like a skunk, you don't play, you go to sleep. (*To Jacoby.*) As for you, seeing him soaked like that, you shouldn't have profited by it. It's immoral!

MELVIL: Bravo!

BOBBY: That's telling them!

MELTCRAFT: (*going to them*) I don't want any trouble in my place.

ARIZONA JACK: (*low to Chick*) When's Nick coming?

CHICK: Patience! It's not yet 4 a.m.! There's still time! He'll come, don't worry.

(*A dispute arises between two women.*)

VAMPIRA: (*furious*) Ah, watch it, Sweets!

SWEETS: (*insolently*) What is it, this time?

VAMPIRA: If you only wink at my man again–

SWEETS: (*sarcastic*) I didn't see your name stamped on his forehead.

VAMPIRA: –I'm going to show you why they call me Vampira.

SWEETS: Don't bother, I know. You're an old bat!

VAMPIRA: You dirty slut!

(*They start pulling each other's hair off. Men intervene to separate them.*)

MELTCRAFT: (*intervening*) None of this fishwife stuff here, understood? What a bunch of shrews! Where do you think you are?

PEDRO: (*shouting*) More champagne!

FRANCIS: Coming, coming!

(*Nick Carter enters made up like Tom Perkins, a.k.a. The Slasher, whose portrait hangs from the wall, but looking ten years older. He holds a stick in his hand and appears like a vagabond dressed in tattered rags.*)

NICK: (*in a powerful voice*) Greetings, friends.

(*Everybody looks at him, stunned.*)

MELVIL: Could it be...?

BOBBY: Nasty face. Who's he?

NICK: Is that the only greeting I'm gonna get? Or don'tcha recognize me? Have I changed that much in 13 years?

MELTCRAFT: (*advancing and respectfully shaking his hands*) Mr. Perkins.

OSWALD: The Slasher.

JACOBY: Yes! It's Perkins.

(*Great curiosity. People stand up to see the newcomer.*)

NICK: Yes, it's me, your former Boss, condemned to life. Just made it out, croaking two guards. (*Sounds of approval and admiration.*) No spies here, I hope? (*Protests.*)

MELTCRAFT: If they were to get in, they wouldn't get out!

NICK: So here you are, my good Meltcraft! Congratulations! You've risen in the world! And you, Otto, you haven't changed–still as plastered as ever!

OTTO: (*shaking his hand*) Good old Tom's back! I'd never have believe it! You've aged a bit, but I'm happy to see you all the same. We did good work together in those days, didn't we?

NICK: And we will again–soon!

SWEETS: (*to Vampira*) Swanky type, eh? If only he scrubbed up a bit.

VAMPIRA: (*admiringly*) He gives me the shivers.

MELTCRAFT: (*pointing to Perkins' portrait*) See here, we didn't forget you. We put you in a fine place.

NICK: Yeah, that's mighty nice, not to forget old friends! You'll put me up for a few days, eh, Meltcraft?

MELTCRAFT: As long as you like, Mr. Perkins.

NICK: My outfit is a bit sloppy. I ask the ladies' pardon. Tomorrow, I'll visit the tailor. I have cash and I'm paying for drinks for everybody.

(*Bravos! Applause, shouts of "Long Live Tom Perkins!" Melvil, who hasn't stopped observing Nick, advances toward him.*)

MELVIL: (*ironic*) Did you make your fortune down in the slammer?

NICK Not quite. But I did a bit of work last night, and I've got nothing to complain about.

MELVIL: I see. Has it been long since you, er, got out for a bit of fresh air?

NICK: A week ago tomorrow, at 11 p.m., I did.

MELVIL: And you croaked two guards? And no one reported it? That's quite extraordinary!

NICK: This gent thinks I should send a note to the papers? Who's this dude?

MELTCRAFT: He's the new Boss.

NICK: The new Boss? Ah, really! So you're my successor? Well, my lad, time to get back in the ranks. I'm the Boss here, and I'm resuming my station.

MELVIL: And I'm keeping mine.

NICK: That's what we're going to see, fella!

MELVIL: It's already seen.

NICK: (*pulling his knife*) Then we're going to settle this right away.

MELVIL: (*drawing his revolver*) If you like.

NICK: Ah! You prefer the gat? It's all the same to me.

MELVIL: No–no shooting. It might be overheard in the street. There's always a bunch of drunks prowling around! (*To Francis.*) You, go lock up upstairs. Put a double bar on the doors.

FRANCIS: Right away, Boss!

(*Francis leaves by the right near the audience.*)

OSWALD: Hold on, there's no reason for the two of you to fight! You were the Boss, Mr. Perkins. Because you were, er, otherwise engaged, we named another. Now you've come back and you're resuming your place, as you say. Nothing could be simpler.

NICK: It seems so to me.

VOICES: Yes! He's right!

MELVIL: Is that's your opinion–all of you?

VOICES: Yes! Yes!

MELVIL: So be it then. (*To Nick/Perkins:*) It seems you're the Boss after all.

VOICES: Bravo! Great!

MELTCRAFT: Come on, drink, the two of you, instead of talking about killing each other.

NICK: I ask nothing more. (*To Melvil:*) Your hand, pal. (*He shakes his hand.*) What's your name?

MELVIL: I'm known as Melvil.

NICK: Melvil? You're Melvil?

MELVIL: Yes.

NICK: (*pushing him away*) In that case, get away from

me! I won't shake the hand of a coward and double-crosser!

(*Stupor of all those present.*)

VOICES: Huh? What did he say? Melvil's a double-crosser? A coward?

MELTCRAFT: For goodness' sake! Mr. Melvil, a double-crosser?

MELVIL: (*disdainfully*) Let him talk, Meltcraft.

NICK: I'm glad to meet you, Melvil! This saves me an errand. My mission is to cut your throat or open your abdomen–your choice.

MELVIL: That's all? And who gave you that mission?

NICK: Someone you know quite well and that I left down there! Surely you haven't forgotten Conegal, Bob Conegal!

(*Melvil shudders.*)

NICK: What's wrong with you, Melvil? You're turning all pale, and green, now!

MELVIL: Me? You're crazy! I don't even know what you're talking about.

NICK: Let everybody hear what I have to say! We're going to judge you, Melvil. And I'm the one who'll take care of the execution.

MELVIL: (*beside himself*) Enough insults! (*He trains his revolver on Nick/Perkins.*)

OSWALD: (*pushing his arm down*) What is it, Melvil? You're afraid?

MELVIL: Afraid? Me?

OSWALD: Then let him talk.

VOICES: Yes, yes, let him talk!

MELVIL: He's an infamous liar.

OSWALD: How do you know what he's going to say? Put your revolver away, Melvil. You'll have your chance to talk later! Speak, Mr. Perkins! What's he accused of?

NICK: I accuse him of betraying our comrade Conegal; of having him delivered into the hands of the police, and getting him condemned to 20 years. All that so he could steal his woman!

(*Melvil shrugs.*)

MELTCRAFT: Carmen?

TOMATO: Yes, it's true. Carmen used to be with Conegal!

OSWALD: What do you say, Melvil?

MELVIL: He's lying.

OSWALD: (*to Nick/Perkins*) It's not enough. You've got to have proof.

NICK: Proof? Here's the proof! I got it from Conegal himself, who was my cellmate down there. He had plenty of time to tell me his story, and I swore to avenge him. You remember the business of the First National Bank when Conegal was caught after having knocked off a guard? (*He addresses himself directly to Melvil.*) You were the one who had the idea of knocking over the bank, and you were the one who led Conegal into it! He went in first, counting on you, but you escaped, like a coward, with the two scoundrels who accompanied you and whom you had treacherously won over! (*Violent murmurs.*) Conegal was caught by the cops and you ran off with his girl! Now that's what you did!

(*Melvil wants to speak but is prevented by shouts.*)

VOICES: Kill him! Kill the rat! Kill the coward. Take him away! Chain him up!

ARIZONA JACK: (*low to Chick*) This is going to be good.

CHICK: (*low*) We've got him now!

BOBBY: Wait! Let him speak!

VOICES: No, no! Kill the traitor!

JIM: Listen to him.

VOICES: No, no!

JIM: He's got a right to defend himself!

VOICES: Kill! Take him out!

ARIZONA JACK: (*letting out his shout*) WHOOP!

(*Nick shivers. Melvil turns abruptly and stares fixedly at Arizona Jack.*)

PATSY: (*aside*) Imbecile!

CHICK: (*aside*) We're lost!

MELVIL: (*bursting into laughter*) Ha! Ha! Ha! A remarkable performance! (*To Nick/Perkins.*) You're not Perkins, are you? No, you're too bold and too good of an actor. You're–Nick Carter!

VOICES: Nick Carter!

MELVIL: Yes, Nick Carter! You've been unmasked! (*Melvil tears off Nick's wig and beard.*) It's you that we're going to judge and I'm the one who'll take care of the execution!

(*Nick pushes Melvil aside and leaps to the platform, revolver in hand.*)

NICK: To me, my friends!

(*Patsy, Chick, Arizona Jack and George also tear off their wigs and beards and leap to the platform.*)

VOICES: Kill them! Let's kill them all! Death to the coppers!

(*The door at back opens and Helen appears, revolver in hand.*)

HELEN: George!

GEORGE: Helen!

MELVIL: To the rings! Forward!

(*Jim and Sam grab Helen. All the villains rush the platform shouting death threats. Shots are fired and several assailants fall, uttering howls of pain. But, eventually, Nick and his friends are overcome, disarmed and tied to the iron collars, their hands tied behind their backs. Several of the dead and wounded are carried out by the door at the right.*)

MELVIL: Now, my friends, pull out your knives and carve these pigs up for me.

HELEN: Stop! (*To Melvil.*) If you touch one of them, I'll kill myself. (*She puts her revolver to her head.*)

MELVIL: Helen!

HELEN: Yes, I'll kill myself, here and now, right before
your eyes! Their lives for mine.

MELVIL: (*after a short hesitation.*) Hold on, comrades.
(*Violent murmurs.*) Those are my orders.
(*More violent murmurs.*) Silence! I am the
master here! Meltcraft, you will untie them
and set them free.

MELTCRAFT: All of them? Even Carter?

MELVIL: (*staring at Meltcraft and carefully weighing
his words*) Yes, all of them. Even Carter.
One by one. (*He points to the Rat Trap.*)
They'll go out through the cellar. You understand me? Through the cellar!

MELTCRAFT: (*he gets it.*) Ah yes. That'll do! (*More
angry murmurs.*) Shut up, you fools. It's a
trick.

MELVIL: (*to Bobby, Jim and Sam*) The rest of you, get
going. (*To Helen.*) Come with me! (*He pulls
her along.*)

GEORGE: Helen! Helen!

HELEN: (*dropping her revolver*) Goodbye!

(*Helen leaves with Melvil, Jim, Sam and Bobby by the
right back.*)

OSWALD: (*with savage delight*) Now, they're ours!

WILLIAMS: We're going to have some fun.

OTTO: It would be too stupid to let them go!

MELTCRAFT: All of you get back! (*low*) Leave this to me. (*aloud*) A promise is a promise. They can leave here safe and sound, one after the other, since that's the Boss's orders. You're free, Nick Carter. (*Meltcraft unties Nick.*)

OSWALD: And don't fall into our hands again!

MELTCRAFT: This time, you don't get cut up.

(*Nick starts heading towards the door at the back right.*)

MELTCRAFT: No. Not that way. It's a secret passage, which must remain secret.

(*Nick goes to the right door, near the audience.*)

MELTCRAFT: Not that way, either. (*He opens the door to the Rat Trap.*) Through the cellar. After 4 a.m., that's the way we leave. (*laughing*) On account of the police! You go down six steps, turn right, and soon you'll find your-self in the courtyard of a nearby house on another street. Understood? Six steps, turn right and there you are! Go!

(*Meltcraft pushes Nick and shuts the door. Everyone listens in silence, as Nick can be heard descending five steps, then utters a great scream of horror. General laughter ensues.*)

OTTO: (*laughing*) He took a plunge.

WILLIAMS: (*laughing*) Into the Rat Trap.

MELTCRAFT: That takes care of one of them!

PATSY: You killed him, bandits!

MELTCRAFT: You bet! (*He looks into the Rat Trap.*) No body left. The rats are going to regale themselves with the excellent Mr. Carter! (*He comes back.*) Now, we're going to gas the others like a mole in its hole. The rest of you, leave. This place is going to become unhealthy.

OTTO: Have a nice night, coppers. A long night.

WILLIAMS: Yeah. Don't have any bad dreams.

JACOBY: Finally, we're rid of that vermin!

(*Everybody leaves by the back right. Meltcraft goes to uncork a canister of gas in the corner at the right back. A little whistle can be heard as the gas escapes.*)

MELTCRAFT: I've turned the spout. Hear it whistle? It's gas! Shut your traps and try not to breathe. It's good advice I'm giving you. I'll be back in an hour to get rid of your bodies. Nighty-night!

(*Meltcraft turns out the light and leaves by the right near the audience. The stage is now plunged into darkness.*)

PATSY: This time, it's over. Ah, the scum!

GEORGE: Helen, my poor Helen!

ARIZONA JACK: Forgive me, my friends!

CHICK: Ah, you can boast of being a real screw-up. Are they all as stupid as you in the West?

(*A short silence.*)

PATSY: My head's spinning! What a dirty death!

CHICK: May God have mercy on us!

(*Suddenly, the door at the left, midstage, opens quietly and Nick Carter enters, holding a flashlight.*)

ALL: Nick Carter!

NICK: Hush!

(*Nick turns the gas off with his handkerchief.*)

CURTAIN

ACT V

Scene VIII. The Red House

A picturesquely furnished room. There is a door at the rear, two side doors midstage left and right and a large fireplace of carved wood at the back left. Back right, there is a large library and back left, a clock on a pedestal, with a gun mounted on top of it. To the right of the clock, there is a large hook at about the height of a man. Near the audience, to the right, there is a small telephone on the wall, with a small table near it.

AT RISE, Melvil is pacing back and forth, making grand impatient gestures. He looks from time to time at the door at the left. Catherine enters from the left.

MELVIL: So?

CATHERINE: Still the same. She hasn't budged since this morning. She slept on top of her bed, fully clothed, face in her hands. She sighs, she weeps. I speak to her and she doesn't respond. Just once, she said to me: "I beg you to leave me alone." All the same, she seems to be getting a little calmer. I think she took a little nap. It's a crisis; it will pass.

MELVIL: She didn't speak to you about the events of
last night?

CATHERINE: No. Not at all.

(*Bobby enters from the right.*)

BOBBY: There it goes, Boss, the machine is sputtering.
If all goes well, we'll have power in an hour.
But there's something that isn't working the
way I'd like.

MELVIL: What's that?

BOBBY: I don't know exactly; I'm not a mechanic! I
hear like a heavy scraping sound and I ask
myself what's going on. It would probably
be good if you were to take a look at it.

MELVIL: I will. What's Jim doing?

BOBBY: He's wiring the torpedoes.

CATHERINE: (*frightened, aside*) Good Lord!

MELVIL: And Sam?

BOBBY: He's placing the detonators. If the electricity
works, no one will get in easily.

CATHERINE: (*trembling*) Can I leave now, Boss?

MELVIL: No, I need you!

CATHERINE: But all that talk of torpedoes and detonators–

MELVIL: Shut up! (*To Bobby*.) Still no word from
Meltcraft?

BOBBY: No, none.

MELVIL: What could it mean? He should guess that I'm
anxious to know what happened! (*He checks
his watch*.) What the Devil! We aren't that
far from New York! He's had plenty of time
to send a messenger.

BOBBY: As for me, I'm not worried. Meltcraft must
have carried out your instructions to the letter. They were clear enough. I think we have
nothing more to fear from Carter.

MELVIL: I hope so, too. But I want to be certain. I'm
going to the engine room.

(*Melvil goes out to the left*.)

BOBBY: (*laughing*) You don't seem reassured, my old
bird.

CATHERINE: You're giving me chills up my spine with
your talk of torpedoes and detonators!

BOBBY: Bah! Forget it! You only die once!

CATHERINE: That's more than enough!

BOBBY: But, you–

CATHERINE: I want to ask you something, Mr. Paddock. A bit of advice.

BOBBY: Yes, my honey-pot?

CATHERINE: When I went for supplies earlier, it seemed to me that I saw Miss Carmen.

BOBBY: (*laughing*) Carmen? You've got to take care of your eyes, my poor old girl! You've got cataracts.

CATHERINE: No, I'd stick my hand in the fire.

BOBBY: It can't be. It's not possible.

CATHERINE: I'm sure I wasn't mistaken. When she spotted me, she turned back abruptly and disappeared down a side street.

BOBBY: Carmen is in the cooler, my girl, and for a good long time.

CATHERINE: Could she have escaped?

BOBBY: Not very likely.

CATHERINE: Still, what do you advise? Should I tell the Boss?

BOBBY: If I were you, I'd watch out! Be like me, never meddle in his love affairs, except to carry out his orders. You've got to be cautious with him. Sometimes he's hot, sometimes he's cold! Today, Carmen is in the soup, tomorrow she may walk on water. And in that case, if you ratted on her, who is gonna pay the piper?

CATHERINE: You're right, Mr. Paddock.

BOBBY: I've always said: a skirt will ruin Mr. Melvil! A shame too! A man like him! Look at you, Kate, you're nice, elegant, pretty–

CATHERINE: (*simpering*) Ah, Mr. Paddock!

BOBBY: No, don't blush, I'm not saying this just for you. Yes, women are delightful, but only for having a good time! As for love, the great, true love–no, thanks. Very little of that for me.

(*Melvil comes back right.*)

MELVIL: (*to Bobby*) The generator's working fine. What were you talking about?

BOBBY: What about that scraping sound?

MELVIL: Just a loose screw.

(*At that moment, the telephone rings, he goes to it.*)

MELVIL: Hello! Hello! Ah, great! Fine. Yes, let him come in. (*hanging up.*) Finally, he's here.

BOBBY: Who?

MELVIL: Meltcraft.

BOBBY: You see? Nothing to worry about.

MELVIL: We'll know what happened.

(*Nick Carter enters at the back, disguised to look like Meltcraft. One side of his face is swollen and purple as if he had received a powerful punch. He wears a bandage.*)

CATHERINE: Mr. Meltcraft! What happened to your face?

BOBBY: You broke your jaw?

MELVIL: Who did that to you?

(*Nick speaks with apparent difficulty, imitating Meltcraft's voice.*)

NICK: It's that damned Nick Carter. May the Devil take his soul! I can barely talk–my tongue's thick as a slug!

BOBBY: My poor friend!

NICK: The brute almost slaughtered me! Anyway, what's certain is that he won't do it again.

MELVIL: You settled his score?

NICK: In style. By now, the rats must have devoured him.

MELVIL: You threw him in the Rat Trap?

NICK: Yes. But that wasn't half of it! It was in the struggle that he punched my clock! Great God! What a blow! He broke three of my teeth and cut off a bit of my tongue.

CATHERINE: Really?

BOBBY: Yeah, it sure looks like it.

MELVIL: And what about the others?

NICK: They're all dead, like their boss. They won't bother you any more.

BOBBY: Poor old Patsy. I didn't suspect that I'd be socking him for the last time. What is it with us mortals? We're truly unimportant creatures.

CATHERINE: (*to Melvil*) The young lady hasn't eaten since yesterday. Should I bring her a bit of soup now? I've got some very good soup in the kitchen.

MELVIL: Yes, try to get her to take some. And be especially careful with your mouth. Not a word

about Carter and the others. Let her suspect
absolutely nothing.

CATHERINE: Don't worry, Boss!

(*Catherine leaves by the back.*)

MELVIL: Good job, Meltcraft. I'm pleased with you.

NICK: Yes, only–see, I haven't told you everything,
Boss.

MELVIL: Ah?

NICK: There were surely other spies at the Rat Trap last
night. And they've been talking...

MELVIL: What makes you say so?

NICK: This morning, at dawn, the cops invaded the bar,
arrested everybody, waiters, sommeliers and
cooks. And I barely had time to escape
through the secret passage. I've been hiding
all morning, and then, I wanted to bring you
the news.

MELVIL: You did well.

NICK: Yes, but I'm ruined! What's going to become of
me?

MELVIL: You'll stay here with us. We'll take care of
you–and you'll help us. There'll soon be
plenty of work here. The police are certainly

going to go after us. It will probably end by them finding their way here, sooner or later.

BOBBY: The risk is great!

MELVIL: Go back to the workshop, Bobby, and watch the pressure.

BOBBY: There's no need to hurry.

MELVIL: It's always better to be ready!

BOBBY: (*to Nick/Meltcraft*) You're not thinking of getting married soon, are you, old friend? No? So much the better! 'Cause with your mug, you wouldn't have an easy time getting registered. Ha! Ha!

(*Bobby goes out by the right.*)

NICK: He pisses me off, that idiot! If we were still at my place–

MELVIL: You'd be pissing him off!

(*Catherine enters at the back carrying a platter with a small soup bowl and a place mat.*)

CATHERINE: Here's the soup.

MELVIL: Find out if she's willing to see me.

CATHERINE: Right now?

MELVIL: Yes.

CATHERINE: Fine!

(*Catherine leaves by the left.*)

NICK: So you're not afraid of the police here?

MELVIL: Not in the least. I'll kill more than a hundred of them before they can even get into the house.

NICK: A hundred?

MELVIL: The garden is mined. The park is full of torpedoes, and powerful electric batteries are connected to the doors and windows.

NICK: Holy cow!

MELVIL: When the power is on, whoever attempts to get in here will fall as if struck by lightning.

NICK: That's shocking. (*laughs*) And the power will be on soon?

MELVIL: In about an hour, more or less.

NICK: And if, despite everything, things go bad? You have to plan for everything...

MELVIL: In that case, we'll escape through a secret passage that is impossible to find and which is only known to me, Bobby and Carmen.

NICK: Hum! Three people in on such a secret. Perhaps that's too many.

MELVIL: Oh, I'll answer for Bobby like myself. And as for Carmen, we won't be seeing her again very soon.

(*Catherine returns carrying the platter.*)

CATHERINE: Useless for me to say or do anything. She won't even taste the soup. She says she's ill. She insists on being left alone.

NICK: (*lifting the lid on the soup pot.*) Christ! It smells delicious. How can anyone turn down a soup like this?

MELVIL: In that case, have some of it. (*laughing*)

NICK: To the last drop. I haven't had anything to eat all day. I can't eat because of my teeth and my tongue; but liquid will go down by itself.

MELVIL: Well! Regale yourself! Sit at this table. (*To Catherine.*) Meanwhile, you, come with me, I've got work for you. A crate of dynamite that you'll carefully unpack for me.

CATHERINE: (*trembling*) Jesus.

(*Nick/Meltcraft sits down and starts slurping the soup.*)

MELVIL: Mr. Meltcraft has got quite an appetite!

NICK: Oh, this soup won't explode!

(*Melvil and Catherine leave. Nick/Meltcraft continues to swallow a few spoonfuls, then stops and quietly goes to the door at the right, passing by the gun-clock, which he studies with some interest.*)

NICK: What a funny clock. And that gun–I wonder what it's for?

(*He continues exploring the room. Suddenly, we hear a choked scream. Nick quickly returns to the table and resumes eating. Helen emerges from her room and stops terrified, seeing Nick whom she believes is Meltcraft.*)

HELEN: Ah!

NICK: (*with a finger on his lips*) Hush! Don't be afraid, It's me, Nick Carter.

HELEN: You! Is it possible?

NICK: (*low, stopping from time to time to listen*) Yes! I'm wearing the face of the odious Mr. Meltcraft in order to inspire confidence to these villains. And as you can see, I've succeeded. (*He rises quickly, goes to listen at the door at the right, then returns.*)

HELEN: And George? What about George?

NICK: George is fine!

HELEN: They freed you after my departure?

NICK: Not exactly. They tried to throw me into the sewers.

HELEN: My God!

NICK: And they tried to gas the others.

HELEN: The wretches!

NICK: But I was suspicious, and thanks to my little flashlight, I avoided plunging to my death. Then, I returned to free our friends. Then we carefully returned to the sewers and escaped by means of an old manhole that was equipped with an iron ladder, and that had been used in the past for cleaning and repairs. (*listening*)

HELEN: How did you know where they'd taken me?

NICK: Very simply. Carmen, Melvil's mistress, was under lock and key. We let her escape, followed her and she led us straight here.

HELEN: Ah! What a frightful night!

NICK: It's all going to be over soon.

HELEN: I pray you're right. Where is George?

NICK: Quite near, with my men and 20 police officers. They're only awaiting my signal to rush this

place and deliver us. Return to your room
and be alert. As soon as you hear Melvil's
voice, call him. Try to be nice to him.

HELEN: Me?

NICK: Yes, you. It must be done. Act appeased, but let
your face show some reserve. He'll be
thrilled. He'll order me to decamp, and while
you detain him, I won't waste any time, I
swear. (*listening*) They're coming. Go back
to your room and be ready.

(*Helen goes back into her room. Nick sits and eats.*)

NICK: (*aside*) Poor little thing. Am I going to succeed?
We're playing our last card!

(*Melvil enters from the left, followed by Catherine.*)

MELVIL: (*to Catherine*) Ah, no! Enough fussing!
You're too ugly when you cry. (*To
Nick/Meltcraft.*) Can you believe that this big
lump is too afraid to touch a stick of dynamite!

CATHERINE: (*blubbering*) I'm too afraid to die.

MELVIL: (*pointing to the platter*) Take away all this
and beat it to your kitchen!

CATHERINE: (*taking the platter*) I'll go crazy, I will, if
I stay in this house!

MELVIL: Tell Jim to come and speak to me as soon as he's finished.

(*Catherine leaves by the rear.*)

MELVIL: Well? Feeling better?

NICK: (*speaking with difficulty*) Yeah. That soup revived me. It's only my tongue which burns like fire. And then my damned broken teeth give me twinges. Maybe the best thing would be to have them yanked out.

MELVIL: Possibly.

NICK: Maybe there's a dentist somewhere in this town...

(*Helen enters from the left.*)

HELEN: Oh, pardon.

MELVIL: (*in a cajoling tone*) Come in, I beg you. Do come in. How are you feeling?

HELEN: Better, thank you. You said you wanted to speak to me.

MELVIL: Yes, indeed. (*To Nick.*) You're right, there's a dentist in town. Go see him. (*He pushes him toward the door at the back.*)

NICK: If not, maybe I can find a doctor?

MELVIL: (*pushing him out*) Yes, yes.

NICK: Or a chemist.

(*Nick leaves by the back.*)

MELVIL: Sit down. (*tenderly*) I beg you. (*slight pause*) Yes, I need to speak to you. Above all, I don't want any misunderstanding between us.

HELEN: I want that as much as you do.

MELVIL: I have the most tender love for you, the most profound passion, and I am suffering wretchedly at the idea that I, who adore you, I, who would give my life for you, am torturing you. I want to conquer you and you detest me. You scorn me.

HELEN: Still, I must tell you that I wasn't expecting such generosity from you. My surprise was great. And if you keep your promise–

MELVIL: I will keep it.

HELEN: I'll be very grateful to you.

MELVIL: (*more and more heatedly*) I will give my life to be worthy of you! Ah, why didn't I meet you sooner? Listen to me, Helen! Don't reject me! Listen to me, you've got to know. I didn't know you. I came into your house under an assumed name, like the thief that I am, to surprise your confidence and rob you. You see, I'm hiding nothing. And beauty took me off guard. After leaving you, I'd go home dazzled, intoxicated, repeating your name to myself in a whisper. And I wept the only tears of my life, thinking about what you were and what I was, and that chasm which separated us! Surely, any hope I might have had was dashed when I discovered you were engaged. But then, I swore that if you couldn't be mine, then you wouldn't be anyone else's! As this thought came to me, it obsessed me. I had to take you, to keep you! And now, you're mine and mine alone! Ah, if you would only give me a chance! No woman has ever been or ever will be loved as I love you! Nothing will cost me too much to give you joy. Say one word, and I will be your slave! Whatever you decide, I will do! Wherever you wish, I will go! No one will be allowed to stand in our way, and just to be near you, just looking at you, will be enough to make me into a different man!

HELEN: (*moved*) I pity you sincerely, and with all my heart!

(*Bobby enters from the back.*)

BOBBY: Sorry, Boss!

MELVIL: (*curtly*) What do you want?

BOBBY: To talk to you.

MELVIL: Later.

BOBBY: (*short and firm*) No, right away.

MELVIL: (*irritated*) Why now?

BOBBY: I've got to. This is serious.

MELVIL: (*after a short pause*) Fine! I'm yours. (*To Helen.*) I beg you to excuse me.

HELEN: (*aside*) Ah, My God! I'm trembling!

(*Helen goes back into her room.*)

MELVIL: Well, what is it?

BOBBY: Come on in, you!

(*He opens the door at the back and Meltcraft enters–the real Meltcraft!*)

MELVIL: Meltcraft?

BOBBY: This one's the real one. He doesn't have his face in tatters. No broken teeth. No cut tongue!

MELVIL: The Devil! And the other one?

BOBBY: It's got to be Carter!

MELVIL: (*furious*) Nick Carter! By Jove!

BOBBY: He's not dead. On account of the fact that Meltcraft here saw him alive and well this morning.

MELVIL: (*to Meltcraft*) You saw him?

MELTCRAFT: At 7 a.m., he came to my place with a dozen cops and arrested my personnel and locked up my shop. I was able to escape through the secret passage.

MELVIL: So he didn't lie to us, after all.

BOBBY: Yes, he had the gall to tell it to our face. Ah, he's got a damned nerve!

MELVIL: (*to Meltcraft*) So what did happen last night after we left?

MELTCRAFT: What happened? I'm still asking myself that! I don't understand a thing!

MELVIL: Why didn't you kill them as I told you? You understood my order, didn't you?

MELTCRAFT: I sure did! I thought I had killed them. I pushed that damned detective into the Rat Trap. We heard him go down five steps, then scream. I checked and there was no one. That man's the Devil himself.

MELVIL: And the others?

MELTCRAFT: The others were tied to the rings. To get rid of them all at the same time, I decided to gas them. I opened the canister and I locked the door. An hour later, when I returned, they were all gone and the canister had been turned off with this handkerchief. (*He pulls the handkerchief from his pocket.*)

MELVIL: (*looking at a monogram*) N.C.

BOBBY: Nick Carter.

MELVIL: So he's the one who rescued them. He must have known of the Rat Trap, anticipated it, freed the others and escaped by the manhole. It's clear.

BOBBY: Where is he now?

MELVIL: He must be prowling around the park and the garden looking for the torpedoes which I foolishly mentioned to him... (*To Meltcraft.*) How did you get in?

MELTCRAFT: Through the small kitchen door.

BOBBY: I'm the one who opened it for him. I noticed him from the attic window. No one else saw him.

MELVIL: Good. If Carter doesn't know you're here, then we can still prevail. You two, go after him and kill him like a dog.

BOBBY: Count on us, Boss. (*To Meltcraft.*) You have your revolver?

MELTCRAFT: Always.

BOBBY: Come with me!

MELTCRAFT: Ah, the dirty copper. He had the nerve to steal my face!

BOBBY: And such a beautiful face, too.

(*They go out by the rear.*)

MELVIL: (*reflective*) What if he's hiding inside the house in order to open the door to his friends when night falls....

(*Jim and Sam enter from the right.*)

JIM: Catherine told us you needed us, Boss.

MELVIL: Yes. Nick Carter is here.

SAM: Nick Carter?

JIM: He's not dead?

MELVIL: That idiot Meltcraft let him escape. Search the house! He may be hidden in some corner. Be suspicious! He's disguised to look like Meltcraft. I was fooled myself. When you've found him, tie him up, gag him, bring him here and hang him on that hook. (*He points*

213

to the hook on the right.) I'll be in the engine room. You'll inform me. Understood?

JIM: Yes, Boss.

MELVIL: There are gags and ropes in this drawer.

(*He goes quietly to Helen's room, locks it and puts the key in his pocket.*)

MELVIL: (*aside*) It's safer that way. (*To Jim and Sam.*) If you catch him, there'll be 200 dollars in it for each of you.

(*Melvil leaves by the right. Sam takes the ropes from the drawer.*)

JIM: Two hundred dollars! All right!

SAM: What'll you do with the money?

JIM: Unfortunately, we haven't caught him yet. It won't be easy. He's Nick Carter.

SAM: Are you afraid?

JIM: Well, there are two of us, I suppose. But let's not get separated, OK?

SAM: You got it.

JIM: Let's go!

(*He leaves by the back; Sam is getting another coil of*

rope and gags when Jim returns precipitously.)

JIM: He's here!

SAM: Carter? You've seen him? Where?

JIM: In the corridor! He's coming. Take the gag, pass
   me the ropes!

SAM: You're sure it's him?

JIM: No mistake. He resembles Meltcraft like two drops
   of water. His spitting image!

SAM: Watch out! I hear him!

(*Jim and Sam hide on each side of the door. The real
Meltcraft enters.*)

MELTCRAFT: I seem to have lost Bobby...

(*Sam jumps and gags him while Jim twists his arms behind his head.*)

SAM: No use struggling, you dirty rat! We have you
   now!

JIM: Bound and gagged!

SAM: Do his legs too!

(*They tie his legs. The gagged Meltcraft makes inar-
ticulate sounds.*)

JIM: Well, what do you say to that, Carter?

SAM: That'll teach you to take the distinguished and sympathetic face of our good friend, Mr. Meltcraft.

(*Meltcraft increases his incomprehensible mutterings.*)

JIM: There he goes howling now! Will you shut up, you dirty mongrel! (*He punches him.*)

SAM: Let's hang him.

(*They tie his hands to the iron ring.*)

JIM: He looks nice, trussed up like a turkey! Can you believe how much he looks like Meltcraft?

SAM: Yeah, it's uncanny.

JIM: Now the clock. (*He goes to the clock.*) Do you know this tool, Carter? No? Well, you'll soon learn. It's what you might call an alarm clock! (*He adjusts the mechanism.*)

SAM: Only, instead of waking you up, bang! it puts you to sleep!

JIM: For a long time!

(*New shouts from Meltcraft.*)

SAM: Shut up, I told you! No one will hear you!

JIM: You see, Carter? It's ten minutes to five. I set the clock for five o'clock. (*He turns a thick steel needle on the dial and sets it on five.*)

SAM: No more than ten minutes to wait, copper. Ah, life is short!

JIM: When five o'clock tolls–

SAM: –You'll check out permanently. (*To Jim.*) Let's tell the Boss.

JIM: Two hundred dollars for each of us.

(*The two leave by the right. Meltcraft makes desperate efforts to scream and break his chains. After several minutes, a section of the library at the back opens, revealing a secret passage from which Carmen emerges.*)

CARMEN: At last, I'm here!

(*Carmen goes to the door of the room at the left and shakes the door in rage.*)

CARMEN: I know she's in here, in my room, the little bitch! In my room!

(*She notices Meltcraft who has done everything he could to attract her attention.*)

CARMEN: Ah, who's this? But–it's Meltcraft!

(*Carmen unties him.*)

CARMEN: What are you doing here? Who bound and gagged you? No, don't answer, I haven't the time.

MELTCRAFT: (*pointing to the clock*) Watch out! The clock!

CARMEN: It's armed?

MELTCRAFT: Yes. Set for five o'clock! Ah, I escaped just in time! Thank you, Miss Carmen! I won't ever forget it. If ever you have need of me–

CARMEN: I do. (*She looks at the clock.*) Five minutes, you say? We've got time.

(*Carmen goes to the door at the left.*)

MELTCRAFT: What do you want me to do?

CARMEN: Break down this door, quick.

(*Meltcraft knocks the door down with his shoulder.*)

MELTCRAFT: There!

(*Carmen rushes inside like a fury and comes out again, dragging Helen behind her.*)

CARMEN: (*to Meltcraft*) Tie her up. Gag her. Hurry up!

(*Meltcraft ties up Helen.*)

HELEN: What have I done to you? I don't know you!

CARMEN: Well, *I* know you. (*To Meltcraft.*) The gag! (*She looks at the clock.*) No more than two minutes now. (*Helen is gagged*) Hang her up, now!

(*Meltcraft attaches Helen to the hook.*)

CARMEN: So long as you live, it's you alone that he wants. So you're going to die. In a minute, I'll be rid of you. And he will love me as he used to, before he met you! For I still love him despite his treacheries. I adore him...

(*The clock starts to strike five.*)

CARMEN: Listen, listen!

(*Second strike.*)

CARMEN: That's your death knell.

(*Third strike.*)

CARMEN: Your death!

(*Melvil enters from the right, followed by Jim and Sam. He takes in everything at a glance. Fourth strike.*)

MELVIL: Helen! No, not you!

(*Melvil places himself in front of Helen, covering her with his body. Fifth strike! There is a powerful detona-*

219

tion. Melvil falls. From the back, Nick enters (without his disguise), followed by Patsy, who leads Bobby who has his hands tied, and several policemen. George Clancy, Arizona Jack and four more policemen emerge from the secret passage.)

CARMEN: (*rushing to Melvil*) My love!

(*Nick unties Helen.*)

BOBBY: Beware of love, Patsy, old boy. And don't pull me so hard!

MELVIL: I loved you, Helen–forgive me!

(*Melvil dies.*)

CARMEN: (*distraught*) It's I who killed him!

(*Helen kneels by the body and prays.*)

GEORGE: Helen! At last! Where is the wretch?

NICK: Forgive him! He died for her.

(*The policemen take Meltcraft, Jim, Sam and a weeping Carmen away. After a brief while, Nick, his assistants, George and Helen, her hand in his, leave, too.*)

(*Suddenly, the corpse appears to mysteriously come back to life and pulls a small metal breastplate from under his shirt.*)

MELVIL: Ha! Ha! You can't get rid of Fantômas that easily! You kept me from the woman I love, and her money too, but I have other plots and plans to ease my pain. I'll be watching you, Nick Carter, and one day, I'll have my revenge.

(*Still laughing, Fantômas, moving stealthily like a panther, goes out through the secret passage.*)

CURTAIN

A postscript about Nick Carter, Fantômas and Zigomar

The authors of the *Nick Carter* stage play were two fairly prolific French vaudevillians, Alexandre Charles Auguste Bisson (1848-1912) and Guillaume Livet (1856-19??). Livet also wrote Harlequin-type novels.

In *Nick Carter*, performed at the Ambigu-Comique Theater in Paris in 1910, the playwrights introduced us to a mysterious villain, the "King of Crime" known only as "Mr. Melvil." It is our contention that this enigmatic character, of which we know nothing, is none other than Fantômas, also known as the "King of Crime" and the "Lord of Terror."

Fantômas made his first literary appearance in February 1911, less than a year after Melvil, when his "biographers," Pierre Souvestre (1874-1914) and Marcel Allain (1885-1970), began publishing his adventures at Librairie Arthème Fayard. It is possible that the earlier appearance of the arch-villain Melvil is only proof that good ideas tend to crop up in various places at the same time. But it is far more likely that Fantômas himself decided that he had picked the wrong writing team to tell his life. After sharing the limelight with Nick Carter in Bisson and Livet's play, the villain preferred instead to entrust his secrets to the more "serious" and journalistic team of Souvestre and Allain.

Fantômas appeared in a total of 32 books written by the two collaborators until Souvestre's death in 1914. He then returned in a subsequent 11 volumes written by Allain alone between 1925 and 1963. He has since become one of the most popular characters in the history of

French pulp literature, inspiring numerous film adaptations (starting with Louis Feuillade's masterful 1913 serials), stage plays, comic books, etc. [3]

*René Navarre as Fantômas
in the Louis Feuillade serials*

What do we know about Fantômas? He appears to have been born in 1867. Souvestre and Allain later revealed that his nemesis, the determined French police detective Juve, was, in fact, his twin brother.

It is established that, on or about 1892, Fantômas, calling himself "Archduke Juan North," operated in the German Principality of Heisse-Weimar. There, he fa-

---

[3] More information about Fantômas can be found in our book *Shadowmen: Heroes and Villains of French Pulp Literature*, ISBN 978-0-9740711-38, Black Coat Press, 2003.

thered a child, Vladimir. In unrevealed circumstances, he was arrested and sent to prison.

In 1895, Fantômas was in India. There, he had an affair with an unidentified European woman, who gave birth to his daughter, Hélène, who was taken to and raised in South Africa. Even though there is some ambiguity about Helen's parentage, Fantômas behaves for all intents and purposes as if she was his daughter.[4]

In 1897, Fantômas went to America, where he met and swindled his business partner, Etienne Rambert. Later, he traveled down to Mexico, then to South Africa where, in 1899, he fought in the Second Boer War under the name of Gurn. He eventually became aide-de-camp to Lord Edward Beltham and fell in love with his young wife, Maud.

In the summer of 1900–before the first novel begins–Gurn and Lady Beltham were surprised in their Parisian love nest by Lord Beltham, who was about to shoot Maud, when Gurn hit him with a hammer and strangled him.[5] Then, Fantômas impersonated Etienne Rambert and framed his son, Charles Rambert, for another murder he had committed. His adversary, Juve, obsessed with his capture, eventually exposed Fantômas and turned Charles into the journalist Jerôme Fandor, working for *La Capitale*.

Lady Beltham remained constantly torn between her passion for Fantômas and her horror at his criminal

---

[4] The story of Helen in South Africa is told in *The Daughter of Fantômas*, ISBN 978-1-932983-56-2, Black Coat Press, 2006.

[5] Italian writer Alfredo Castelli provided a new perspective on this incident in his short story "Long Live Fantômas" in *Tales of the Shadowmen 3: Danse Macabre*, ISBN 978-1-932983-77-7, Black Coat Press, 2007.

schemes. She eventually committed suicide in 1910 after killing the son of one of Fantômas' earlier victims who was seeking revenge. Fandor fell in love with Hélène and, despite Fantômas' repeated attempts to break them up, married her. Fantômas' evil son, Vladimir, reappeared in 1911 and was shot by Juve, just as he was about to kill Hélène.

According to *La Fin de Fantômas*, both Fantômas and Juve were reputed to have died aboard the *Titanic*–transparently renamed the *Gigantic*–in 1912. However, the return of Fantômas is well documented by Allain himself and other authors.[6]

There are numerous pieces of evidence that lead us to believe that the villainous Mr. Melvil of Bisson and Livet's *Nick Carter* and Fantômas are one and the same man.

For a start, there is Fantômas' well-established connection with America. We already know that he spent some time there in 1897. During that time, he was able to build a criminal organization that served him well later in several instances:

• In August 1901, Fantômas was able to arrange for the explosion of the ship *Lancaster* which carried the real Etienne Rambert from the U.S. back to France.

• In June 1902, after one of Fantômas' many identities was exposed by Juve, the villain and Lady Beltham

---

[6] Marcel Allain's sequels, Bill Cunningham's story "Trauma" and Jess Nevins' story "A Jest to Pass the Time" in Tales *of the Shadowmen 2: Gentlemen of the Night*, ISBN 978-1-932983-60-9, Black Coat Press, 2006; as well as David White's forthcoming novel, *Fantômas in America* (based upon the 1920 American serial), all presuppose Fantomas' continued survival.

were forced to flee France and sought refuge in America, returning only a year later.

• In May 1905, the American detective Tom Bob (another of Fantômas' many aliases) arrived in France aboard the ship *Lorraine*.

• In 1907, while hiding in London under the double disguise of "Tom Bob" and "Dr. Garrick," Fantômas took a mistress; to protect her from his enemies (including the jealous Lady Beltham), he tried to send her to America.

• In December 1909, just before the events of Bisson and Livet's play, Fantômas had to flee France again and was in America. According to Allain and Souvestre, he then plotted to steal a fortune in gold being transported on the ship *Triumph* from the East Coast of the United States to the harbor town of Cherbourg in Normandy.[7]

All the events described above make it clear that, throughout his nefarious career, Fantômas considered America as one of his safe havens. He also relied on the help of a powerful network of American criminals, whether to blow up a ship or create a deep cover such as that of Tom Bob.[8]

Bisson and Livet's play states that Melvil has quite

---

[7] Fantômas returned to America in January 1912 for one more battle with Juve, at the end of which the detective killed Fantômas' son, Vladimir. Two months later, Fantômas, pursued by all the forces of police of Europe, looked again to America for refuge and embarked on the *Titanic*.

[8] Tom Bob is an American detective with whom Juve had once fought a gang of anarchists; obviously, the real Tom Bob was killed by Fantômas' American accomplices in order for the villain to take his place.

a criminal record in America and crossed swords with Nick Carter before. It also establishes that Melvil took over a criminal gang from another villain, Tom Perkins, a.k.a. The Slasher, who is serving time in jail. This is the same methods that Fantômas used successfully in Europe.

Melvil's twisted passions for Carmen and Helen Dodler are entirely in accordance to what we know of Fantômas' nature. His possessive obsession for Lady Beltham is boundless; yet, while in England he had an affair with Françoise Lemercier

Finally, the name "Melvil" itself could be construed as a contraction of "Mal-Evil," a fitting alias for the one, true Lord of Terror.

Perhaps inspired by the success of his *Nick Carter*, Guillaume Livet went on to pen two more garish thrillers featuring unusually sadistic evil masterminds: *Pietro Darena, le Semeur de Morts* (Pietro Darena, The Sower of Death) and *Miramar, l'Homme aux Yeux de Chat* (Miramar, The Man with Cat's Eyes) both published by Tallandier, respectively c. 1910-12.

Pietro Darena is a mad doctor and a serial killer. Moved by an insane desire for vengeance, he slaughters his victims in unusually gruesome ways, reflecting the influence of the then-popular *Grand Guignol* plays by André de Lorde. Eventually, a remorseful Darena ends up in a lunatic asylum. Miramar is a mad scientist out to conquer the world. He combines Fantômas' criminal aspirations, the Nyctalope's superhuman abilities (he can see in the dark with his cat-like eyes) [9] and Dr. Cor-

---

[9] For more about The Nyctalope, see *The Nyctalope vs. Lucifer*, ISBN 978-1-932983-98-2, Black Coat Press, 2007.

nelius' passion for performing mad surgery on his victims.

Fantômas made his transition to the silver screen in 1913 when Louis Feuillade (1873-1925) began to make a series of remarkable serials for Gaumont: *Fantômas*, *Juve contre Fantômas*, *Le Mort qui Tue* (all 1913), *Fantômas contre Fantômas* and *Le Faux Magistrat* (both 1914). But prior to these, both Nick Carter and Fantômas' predecessor and rival, the "King of Thieves" known as Zigomar,[10] had already enjoyed their first silent movie adventures at the hands of French pioneer filmmaker Victorin-Hippolyte Jasset (1862-1913). Between 1908 and 1913, Jasset produced serials featuring Nick Carter and Zigomar, separately and together.

Nick Carter, le roi des détectives, co-written with Georges Hatot (1876-1959), was comprised of six episodes: 1: *Guêt-apens* (The Trap); 2: *L'affaire des bijoux* (The Affair of the Jewels); 3: *Les faux-monnayeurs* (The Counterfeiters); 4: *Les dévaliseurs de banque* (The Bank Robbers); 5: *Les empreintes*  (The Fingerprints) and 6: *Les bandits en habits noirs* (The Black Coats). Pierre Bressol (1874-1925) was cast as Nick Carter. Bressol went on to play the character of rival detective Nat Pinkerton in a 1912 serial, and later, became a noted film director.

The success of this first serial encouraged Jasset to make *Les Nouveaux exploits de Nick Carter* in 1909, comprised of two episodes: 1: *En danger* (In Danger)

---

[10] Created by Léon Sazie for the newspaper *Le Matin* in 1909.

and 2: *Le sosie* (The Lookalike). Bressol reprised his role, working alongside Maryse Dauvray, Madeleine Grandjean, Cécile Guyon and Charles Krauss.

Then followed four stand-alone *Nick Carter* shorts: *Les dragées soporifiques* (The Sleeping Pills), *Le club des suicidés* (The Suicide Club) (both 1909), *Nick Carter acrobate* (Nick Carter Acrobat) (1910) and *Le mystère du lit blanc* (The Mystery of the White Bed) (1911), again with Bressol.

That year, Jasset decided to switch sides, so to speak, and tackle the hugely popular character of crime-lord Zigomar. Zigomar is the leader of a criminal gang of gypsies who hides his face beneath a scarlet hood. His nemesis is a Nick Carter-influenced French detective named Paulin Broquet. In *Zigomar, roi des voleurs* (King of Thieves) (1911), Zigomar was played by Alexandre Arquillière, his paramour La Rosaria by Josette Andriot and the fearless Broquet by André Liabel. Another Zigomar serial followed immediately, entitled simply *Zigomar* (1911) (a.k.a. Zigomar the Eelskin) with the same cast and–surprise!–a cameo appearance by Nick Carter, played by Charles Krauss! The stage had been set for a clash of the titans, which occurred the following year in *Zigomar contre Nick Carter* (1912), pitting Zigomar-Arquillère against Carter-Krauss.

Zigomar made one further appearance in the three-parter *Zigomar, peau d'anguille* (Zigomar the Eelskin) (1913) (not to be confused with the 1911 serial), comprised of: 1: *La résurrection de Zigomar* (The Resurrection of Zigomar); 2: *L'éléphant cambrioleur* (The Elephant Burglar) and 3: *Le brigand de l'air* (The Aerial Bandit).

Nick Carter, on the other hand, did not return to the French screens until 1964 and 1965 in, respectively, *Nick Carter va tout casser* (Nick Carter Unleashed, a.k.a. License to Kill) and *Nick Carter et le trèfle rouge* (Nick Carter and the Red Club), where the character was played by Eddie Constantine as a French James Bond substitute.

Jean-Marc Lofficier

231